The Beauty of Men Never Dies

Terrace Books, a trade imprint of the University of Wisconsin Press, takes its name from the Memorial Union Terrace, located at the University of Wisconsin-Madison. Since its inception in 1907, the Wisconsin Union has provided a venue for students, faculty, staff, and alumni to debate art, music, politics, and the issues of the day. It is a place where theater, music, drama, literature, dance, outdoor activities, and major speakers are made available to the campus and the community. To learn more about the Union, visit www.union.wisc.edu.

The Beauty of Men Never Dies

An Autobiographical Novel

David Leddick

Terrace Books
A trade imprint of the University of Wisconsin Press

I would like to acknowledge the great assistance of **Jose Lima** and **William Spring**, my friends and editorial advisors, who have done so much in the creation of this book.

Terrace Books
A trade imprint of the University of Wisconsin Press
1930 Monroe Street, 3rd Floor
Madison, Wisconsin 53711-2059
uwpress.wisc.edu

3 Henrietta Street
London WC2E 8LU, England
eurospanbookstore.com

Printed in the United States of America

Library of Congress Cataloging-in-Publication Data

Leddick, David.
The beauty of men never dies: an autobiographical novel / David Leddick.
        p.   cm.
ISBN 978-0-299-29270-6 (cloth: alk. paper)
ISBN 978-0-299-29273-7 (e-book)
1. Older gay men—Fiction.
I. Title.
PS3562.E28444B43   2013
813'.54—dc23
2012043338

This book is for

Eduardo Goicolea

who prepared me for and has kept me going through these later years

Contents

The Beauty of Men Never Dies

The Beauty of Men Never Dies

There was always thunder in the distance that summer. And an occasional flash of lightning on the edge of the world. *Do you ever have the feeling that everything that has been routine isn't routine anymore?* That the foundations and rhythms are not necessarily worse or better, but different? I felt that way that summer in Miami Beach when instead of tropical heat and blinding sun we had constant small traveling storms.

In the morning walking the dogs it wasn't still and suffocating but more like one of those New England mornings where the air is warm, the sky is a soft gray, a slight wind is turning the leaves upside down, and all the greenery has a fine black edge to it. The kind of morning when you should be running through tall grass and falling in love with the wrong person. The morning of a Brontë novel.

The weather prepared me for what was to come. Of course, everyone was worried about global warming. Everyone but the president and his pals, who were somehow counting on God to pull us through. The ice caps are melting, the sea is rising, soon all this valuable Miami Beach property will be underwater. And so on and so on. I always wonder why people are so concerned about their public lives and so unconcerned about their private lives. I am not worried about what will happen to the world with the rising tides. I am worried about whom I am going to sleep with. Coming from the 1930s Depression, as a child my greatest fantasy was to live in France and speak French. Which I did as a TV director in my early forties. The rest has been dessert.

I would like to say, however, that this is just about work—which was always second to romance for me. All I really wanted was a great love affair and I have been very fortunate. I never wanted a domestic life, as my observations were that fulfillment did not lay in that direction. I have been truly fulfilled, though homosexual, and at the moment am very much involved with someone much younger than myself and have a sex life. My goal is to have a sex life until I am ninety. If I can achieve that then I feel I can say my life was a success.

I am seventy-seven and life does not seem to move rapidly for me, as many find as they get older. I feel that I have been seventy-seven for several years. Just yesterday as I was walking the dog in the morning I heard my neighbor's outdoor caged birds calling. And I thought, *We have spent our lives in this beautiful cage. No wonder we are afraid to be free.*

But who knows what wonders await us? Out there.

I think no one is satisfied with his life if he has not successfully loved, and by that, I mean getting laid and the rest of it. We pursue all kinds of grandiose schemes to control our lives, and particularly the lives of others, via war or religion, but it is really a result of not successfully connecting with another human being. That is why I dislike homophobia. How can anyone feel they have the right to deny another person completion?

And I wonder if at seventy-seven I will ever sleep with anyone else again, though suddenly there are so many likely prospects. Or should I call them unlikely prospects?

I remember reading an interview with a woman ceramicist well known for her pots and bowls. She was in her nineties, living somewhere like Taos, New Mexico, vamping about in a sari and lots of jewelry. The interviewer asked her if she still worked, and she said, "I must throw pots every day or I'd do nothing but think about young men." Her name was Beatrice, I believe. I dismissed it at the time, but now I think about it more.

In her memoirs, M. F. K. Fisher remembers a young plumber or carpenter being in her home when she was much older and feeling some kind of electricity between them. That is the grave problem when you are older. Are you feeling something, or are you imagining it? And is this young or younger person simply turning on their sexually charged charm for you as they do all the world, or is something happening?

I think when you are older you automatically consider yourself to be imagining some kind of attraction if you are still in command of your senses. You look in the mirror and say to yourself, "Although well preserved, this cannot be attractive to another human being in a sexual or romantic way." You base this on your own experience, wondering if you were ever capable of hankering for an older person yourself, and you tell yourself a resounding "no."

But then again, you are not the world. It is possible that there are people out there who have emotions that are different from yours. I keep telling myself that but I have never encountered such people. Or perhaps I have and dismissed them.

There are bars where older gay men go to meet younger men. There is a fiction in the gay world that younger men, some of them, are very attracted to older men. The younger men I have met and seen with older men are always quite obviously there for the advantage of money, security, education, those kinds of things. I have made a rule not to go about with a younger man who is interested in me unless he is a millionaire. In that way at least other people can rest assured that it's not for money.

I think people have an exaggerated idea of how much money I have anyway. And I have for the most part been able to distance myself from young men who may fake romantic interest. Except for that very unfortunate period in my fifties, I have been crazily in love but always with someone roughly in my age range.

My tragedy, if one can call it that, is that I have lived my life for the dramatic and meaningful love relationship. And now I have grown too old for that. And still it is all I know or want. Really, all that I was made for.

It is true. And I have had to battle many times to find fulfillment. Only one of my loves wanted to love me before I wanted to love him.

Not that there haven't been men who wanted to love me without my goading. But I have not wanted to love these men in return. I remember one young man, many years ago now but I was certainly ten years older than he was even then, saying, "I can't believe I'm lying here with my arms about you." It was on a couch in a ground-floor apartment in

Greenwich Village in New York. The windows gave directly onto the street. One lover of mine used to like leaping through the window, Errol Flynn style. It was a Grove Street address on Sheridan Square.

Toward the end of my tenure in that apartment, I remember a friend dropping in and saying, "Strangers in the bedroom, an old boyfriend in the bathroom; this is like the old days." He was referring to the fact that in my first days in that apartment, between the Seventh Avenue subway line and the Sixth Avenue stop, everyone I knew dropped in with great regularity. Some to use the bathroom, some for a drink of water or just a drink, some to try to lay their hands on me for a while. As my dancer friend Bobby said once, "You tall, difficult blonds always get your own way. We short brunettes just get our brains fucked out." And even that ended for Bobby. I'm still supporting him and we weren't even friends when we were dancing together in shows.

Lovers

I always thought I would have four major lovers. Four is my lucky number. And forty-four. And fourteen. Forty-four was the number of my football jersey, if you can imagine me playing football. I often see the building number 44 when I am traveling down a street in a taxi. Just jumps out at me. And although my third major lover and I severed our connection quite a long time ago, and there have been a number of abortive efforts since, I was never concerned. I just always felt number four would show up sooner or later. And he did.

My first lover was the blond god. His name was Clyde. We met in the navy. He wasn't really gay except he fell in love with me. But I haven't forgotten that he was frequently the one who made the first move to some new sex kink. He eventually married and has children.

The second one lasted for thirty years. He wasn't really a blond god. He was more a Greek god. You have to say this for my lovers: they have all been very handsome. I don't know if I ever really loved him. I had this big sexual crush on him that lasted for three decades. I never didn't feel like sleeping with him, even after thirty years. He never really got his life together. And then he died. He had pretty well worn out my emotions for him by that time.

The third lover was the great love of my life. He was smaller, darker, Italian. I always said of him, "When you got fucked by him, you stayed fucked for a while." Strange, isn't it? The way a person makes love can sort of make up for everything else. I really loved him. I would get very excited in a taxi just because I was on my way to meet him. That's real love.

7

And now there has been the fourth one. I used to say to him, "I love you very much." And he would reply, "That's what my wife would always say." So I stopped saying it. So this is being over seventy and being in love with someone far younger. Does this younger lover really want you to be in love with him?

Role Models

There are no role models for gay men as they enter their seventies.

Cecil Beaton perhaps. Although he was awfully swish, and I could never handle those big tip-tilted hats he affected.

No, gay men as they age seem to remain forever attracted to the young. Their escaping youth? It's not pretty. The sour ones who feel life disappointed them turn to alcohol to soften their sorrow. You see them everywhere.

Then there are the aging gay couples who occupy the standard marital position of being with someone you don't particularly care about, which makes it impossible for you to meet someone you might really care about. That's another possible destiny.

And there are the wealthier ones with the much younger lover whom they blissfully believe love them for themselves. Perhaps. But I always point out to my wealthy friends that you never see one of those youths falling in love with an older man who has no money.

None of these possibilities look very attractive to me. How could they? I have had to find role models among women. I have Chanel and Elsie de Wolfe, also known as Lady Mendl.

Coco Chanel returned to her career as a *coutouriére* after World War II at seventy and prospered for almost two more decades. I often quote her saying, "I never designed a good dress until I didn't care anymore." I understand that perfectly and had to in my long years in advertising. You knew what a good job was and you did it. What others thought was not a deciding factor. That is being professional.

Continuing on doing something you know how to do seems a viable activity in your seventies. What is it people wish to retire to do? I am not tired. Perhaps someday when I realize I am tired to a point where I will never feel rested again I will stop and sit down. Then my Zen studies will save me. I will sit on a cushion in the corner staring at the wall, and no one will know that I am actually senile. They'll just say, "He's meditating."

A number of the highly placed Zen masters whom I knew were alcoholic. They just sat there completely stewed and stared into space. As good an example for aspiring Zen students as any. One told me, "I just couldn't do it any other way." Those endless days and nights stretching into weeks just sitting there. *Plunk.*

Elsie, Lady Mendl, is my other role model. She had been the actress Elsie de Wolfe living with Bessie Marbury, a major theater producer at the turn of the twentieth century. Elsie was a society girl with no money but good taste. Every year she went to Paris and bought a wardrobe that she then displayed in a new play, produced by Bessie. They lived together but perhaps Elsie never delivered her slender body to ponderousness. Bessie was big and fat. Women were fond of cuddling and hugging a lot in those days. Mark Twain said he didn't want to go to heaven because everyone was going there to "hug and hug and hug and hug." I used to turn my nose up at this, but lately I don't know.

When Elsie was in early middle age she abandoned her theater career, which was primarily designed to sell tickets to dressmakers who would come and feverishly sketch her outfits. In this way fashion came to New York from Paris. But Elsie was getting too old. So she turned her taste into a whole new kind of career as an interior decorator. It hadn't really existed before. She was a big hit. She introduced painted woodwork in light colors, did away with heavy draperies, lightened things up overall, and made a lot of money with commissions from wealthy women. Then during World War I, she went to France as head of a volunteer nurses' unit. She was awarded a medal by the French government and met and married Lord Mendl, who was attached to the British Embassy in Paris. He was quoted as saying, "The old girl could still be a virgin for all I know."

Elsie blazed on, now as Lady Mendl, through the twenties and thirties. She did not lose money in the crash. All her money was in her jewels. Never pretty, she regularly had facelifts and stood on her head daily. She would also do her headstand and a cartwheel as a party trick while wearing the new fashion slacks made popular by Chanel. Elsie would say, "The important thing is to remain supple." How true.

Elsie groomed Wallis Warfield Simpson for her role as the king of England's mistress. She made the faintly vulgar Wallis into an impeccable fashion symbol and did her job so well the king gave up his throne for Wallis.

When World War II came Elsie fled Paris with her husband, her secretary, her chauffeur, and her jewelry, paying for the gas as they headed for the Spanish border with charms from her gold charm bracelet. She got the whole group, car and all, onto a ship out of Lisbon and proceeded from New York to Hollywood. There she relaunched her career as a decorator very successfully. She was certainly in her seventies by then.

After the war, she returned to her villa in Versailles and raged on as a famous hostess and decorator until her death. Who wouldn't want to do that?

My only problem is that I would certainly want to include a sex life, and as a gay man I have that privilege. But I certainly don't want to pay for it. At least not on a per-session basis. Never have I yet, although the hired escort is a staple of many older gay men's lives. And many younger ones, too.

So here we are. Without role models. What kind of a life can a gay man in his seventies lead to set an example for younger men?

As I entered my seventies, I perceived that the two métiers in which age mattered less were writing and the theater. The writing I had already embarked upon and the theater came upon me unexpectedly. But I have found it to be true. Even if you are rich you will be looked upon as an old fart not really worth knowing by younger people. If you are well known as a writer, however, it makes you somehow ageless. And if you are a performer in the theater, you seem to become what Cocteau said when asked his age: "A legend has no age."

Fenil

I am such a silly cunt. I think there is every possibility of my becoming interested in a twenty-one-year-old Uruguayan policeman. In my midseventies. How can I possibly do something that I find so embarrassing in my aging friends who are infatuated with much younger men? Much younger. I can handle someone in his fifties, and even that is twenty-plus years younger.

His name is Fenil. It sounds like "fennel." He says he has no idea where his mother dreamed it up. Would it be too weird to say Fenil seems to be revolving into my life like some kind of destiny object? Something like those Swiss weather clocks people used to have when I was a child—a little Swiss chalet on the wall with two archways. A man came out when it was going to be fair and a woman when it was going to be rainy. Or perhaps the other way around. I haven't thought of them in years. I wonder how they worked and whether they exist anywhere anymore. Well, Fenil is a little bit like the Swiss weather clock. He's appearing like clockwork, but is that forecasting good weather or bad?

I have been in Montevideo for a month. The guests have been non-stop and I have been a familiar face in all my favorite restaurants and watering holes. The top of the Radisson Hotel. Panini on the Calle de Bacacay. The Café Bacacay at the other end of that street. El Viejo y El Mar (The Old Man and The Sea) down on the Rambla approaching Pocitos. One of the few waterside restaurants in this city built entirely on beaches. Strange, no?

My guests and I have also been up and down the coast. Out to Punta del Este, that sort of frightening small replica of Miami Beach. The more front-edge La Barra with all its blondes in sporty vehicles with radios blaring. On out to José Ignacio, which is a tiny town on a tiny promontory where you could walk all over town on the tops of cars, the streets are so congested. Then up to La Paloma, a little dusty with one good restaurant. Why is it touted as being the fashion destination for next year? Then to Pedrera, which is also congested with Argentineans and is far prettier on its cliff with two beaches sweeping down on either side.

Fenil is a policeman and as such was guarding Adriana's brother, who was in the pokey. Adriana is my manager in Uruguay. She was raised in the United States until the age of fourteen and speaks perfect English. She is also very smart. Adriana, who is beautiful, responsible, and the solid brick core of her family, has a wild brother who has been roaming about the United States for a long time. Long enough to father two children by two different brides and now may be selling something illicit in Los Angeles. Adriana says Cuban cigars. I wonder . . .

I also wonder if he was really put in jail while visiting his family here because he offered a bribe to an office worker to expedite the renewal of his citizenship papers. Uruguayans have citizenship identity cards that require renewal. He was in this country for that, offered someone a bribe because he wanted to return to L.A. quickly, and was seized and placed in the vast and Hitlerian jail just up the street from me.

Conditions in the jail are more collegiate than penal, it seems. Adriana had to bring him a mattress. The jail does not provide that. She took one from one of her children's beds (it was the weekend and stores were closed). In a few days, her brother requested another longer one as the jail was being inspected by a newspaper and the warden had asked that the inmates get new bedspreads and curtains for their suites. Three men to a room, to avoid hanky-panky, I suppose, and with rather nice bureaus, mirrors, closets, etc. I saw pictures.

There was also a kitchen on each floor, and Adriana's brother had appointed himself chef for the floor and requested large amounts of rice, beans, and other foodstuffs. Neither Adriana nor her mother have incomes to speak of but had to provide the food as their brother and son explained that this was how he stayed on the right side of the other prisoners.

During this period of crisis, Adriana's mother met Fenil at the jail, where he was guarding prisoners. Did she perceive that he was attractive? That he had a good body? She was the one who suggested Fenil contact the photographers who were looking for nude models. They were friends of mine visiting Montevideo. They wanted some nude male models for a book they were working on. I suggested they contact Adriana, as I was in Miami at the time. Evidently Adriana discussed it with her mother, and Mom did the rest. Fenil turned out to be a good model for my friends, legs ajar on the red Victorian settee in my home, where the photographers were staying. I wondered, too, when I saw the photos, if my photographer friends had gone further than the pictures with Fenil. But I was not particularly interested in meeting him. A so-so model, I concluded.

Later, when I was in Montevideo, Fenil showed up for dinner with yet another acquaintance from Miami. I was a little surprised. Fenil was uninvited and unexpected. He was just accompanying the man, more a friend of the photographers than mine. I knew this man was no stranger to paying for escort services and imagined that the photographers had recommended Fenil to him.

During dinner I had mentioned that I was looking for a gym in my neighborhood, and Fenil said there was one directly across from the police station and that he would take me there. He gave me his name and number, and in the flood tide of guests coming and going I lost it. And now, weeks later and the last houseguest only gone for about fifteen minutes, the doorbell rings. And there, like the little weather figure revolving into my life, was Fenil and his red bicycle inquiring if I was at home and would like a little visit.

Fenil wears glasses, which is one of my weaknesses when it comes to sexy men. He is not tall. He is not slender. He is muscular but does not emphasize it, wearing loose clothes and long pants, even on his bicycle, I noticed. This was also a plus. Fenil pulled up his shirt to fan his body a bit as he walked around the courtyard. His stomach and lower ribcage were flat, as was the fine dark hair that made a feathery pattern there.

I was tired, and the effort of speaking Spanish and finding my way through his television-acquired English made my heart sink. But I got him a Diet Coke, and we chatted sitting beside each other on one of the couches. I wondered if this was one of those scenarios where a younger man drops by to see if an older man is interested in a little blowjob (to be given by the older man to the younger man, obviously) for a disproportionate amount of money. There was something horny going on with Fenil, and I could feel some interest in him on my part. Which did not please me at all. I really had hoped that my disastrous outing in my fifties with someone who was very inappropriate in age and income would be it. And it still may be.

So Fenil and I went to the gym together. A very sad place right across from the Third Reich–style police station. Up one flight with low ceilings, a sad gray light to match the worn gray carpeting. The workout equipment had never been first-class and was badly knocked about now. There seemed to be exactly one complete set of weights.

I did Fenil's weight training program with him. First, he did a set of weights, then I did. Some of the time I could use the same weights he did. Fenil was surprised. He looked at me at one point and said, "How old are you?" in a kind of mocking way. All the time I'm searching for clues about whether he is a simple kid, a little hustler on the way up, or a manly young guy for his age. "Old," I said. "Very old."

Fenil's arms are not overly big, considering the weights he can handle. When he leaned back on a semi-upside-down position, a surprisingly large bulge pushed forward from his crotch. I didn't remember it being out of the usual in his naked photographs. When he stood up and did weights over his head with his back very flat, his buttocks pushed into his gym pants and looked large and firm. I'm avoiding the word "inviting."

Without his glasses, Fenil's eyes seemed larger and more luminous and his mouth wetter and redder and less sharply formed. In his heritage, there is something that exudes more heat and spontaneity than found in Northern Europeans. The switch was flipped, and the current was on. There was that feeling that I was slipping into emotions that really weren't mine to control. I was loath to stamp out the brushfire when I didn't expect ever to be caught up in another one.

We finished, and Fenil had to hurry on his way, as he had to report for duty supervising the big Mardi Gras parade that evening. I had rented a balcony over Isla de Flores Street and had invited friends. I would rather have been with Fenil, let's face it.

I wanted to pay him something, and he said I should decide on a fee. I said, "One hundred pesos?" and gave him a two-hundred-peso note, all I had. "That's for next time, too," I said. We agreed to meet at four on Monday, right after his tae kwon do class. I decided I should give him two hundred pesos a class. That's still only eight dollars.

A Dream

Idreamed last night I was walking on a wide stretch of beach with Ricky, my childhood lover. We were lovers from when we were very small children through our teen years. He was always going to marry me.

As we walked we could see white clouds piled high before us, with an opening at horizon level, through which the setting sun shone. I could feel Ricky's penis against me from behind as we walked, and I anticipated that sometime before long he would be within me.

As we looked at the horizon, there was a beautiful sailing ship turning in the wind. It was much more like a Maxfield Parrish painting than anything one might actually see in nature.

We were walking across the sand toward low-lying buildings that were film studios where I was going to work. Ricky was accompanying me. As we approached the buildings, there was a group of people posed in the sand, framed by an aperture in the clouds on the horizon beyond them. They were all in white. Again, it was very beautiful and very Maxfield Parrish.

As I slowly awoke, I thought that perhaps it was a flash forward as to what heaven might be like. And then I thought that it was more certainly what I might imagine heaven to be like.

Ricky has been dead for a decade at least, and we never saw each other as adults. We had a relationship where our bodies loved to make love, although I was never in love with him as I was to be with other men later. It was a kind of love relationship but not a romantic one. Perhaps the kind people had before they learned about romantic love in the nineteenth century.

The Day I Knew
Everything Wasn't Going
to Turn Out All Right

My father died in the night shortly
before my twelfth birthday. He had been ill with cancer for years, but I
didn't really expect him to die. No one I knew had.

My next-older brother, Andrew, woke me in the morning. He was
smiling. He said, "Daddy died last night," triumphant that he knew
something I didn't know. He always had an unpleasant personality in
the family. In the world outside, he was all charm. I don't think I ever
really liked him again after that morning.

When I went downstairs, my grandmother was sitting in a chair
weeping, and I knew what my brother had told me was true. My mother
said nothing to me about my father's death nor did she ever.

To test the waters I dressed for school and said to my mother, "I'm
going to school now." I knew you didn't go to school until after the
funeral if someone in your family died. My mother said, "You're not
going anywhere." And then a neighbor woman arrived, and I saw my
mother and her go into my father's bedroom to change the bed. He was
definitely not there. That was all my mother ever said to me about my
father's death. But after that I knew death would always be hovering.
Which it still is.

The Night I Definitely Knew
Everything Wasn't Going
to Turn Out All Right

In the high school that I attended it was the custom for students to go to the movies on Sunday night. Our only movie theater was in the town across the river—a theater that had been built for amateur theatricals before World War I and then adapted to show motion pictures.

The bill changed three times a week, with the major new movie screening on Sunday, Monday, and Tuesday. The rest of the week was largely double bills of B-movies.

Students who were social went to the screenings on Sunday because it was the first evening of the newest and best film of the week.

As World War II was ending, many of us were there in a chatty, cheerful mood. Middle-class kids who worked after school, we had our own money to spend, and we hadn't paid all that much attention to the war. When the newsreels that preceded every movie came on, the footage was of American troops entering the concentration camps. Now the world knows. Then no one had any idea of the cruelty the Germans had inflicted upon their Jewish, gypsy, political, gay, and other hostages. The living skeletons in their striped clothing clung to fences and stared at the camera. Bodies that were nothing but bones were stacked up like cordwood. And it was immense. The haunted faces went on and on and on.

It wasn't so much horrifying as unthinkable. I don't remember that we discussed it after the feature was over. And I don't know what impression it made on my friends. My reaction was: "So. People are capable of that." I realized that taking care of myself in the world was going to be a bigger project than I had realized. The earth felt shaky under my feet. It has never really felt firm since.

After I saw those newsreels I remembered the worst thing I have ever said. I was a silly teenager, if that is any excuse, and a woman from a nearby city asked me if I knew a girl in the class above me in school. I responded, "That little Jew?" Why I would have done this I cannot say. I didn't know that the family was Jewish. Her brother was one of my closest friends. I must have heard some discussion somewhere and thought it was a sophisticated, adult reaction. It turned out the woman worked in the same office in the nearby city with the girl's mother. I felt ashamed immediately and have very regularly since. Where would this kind of anti-Semitism have come from in my provincial, rural world?

Falling in Love Again

I think I am with someone totally inappropriate. If he was any younger he could be my great-grandchild, let alone grandchild. All I have to cling to is Jennie Jerome Churchill, Winston Churchill's mother. Her second husband was thirty or forty years younger than she was.

I need a role model like that. Not someone like Christian Dior, who died at an Italian fat farm trying to lose weight in order to be worthy of his new African lover, much younger than himself.

As far as Fenil is concerned, I am trying to grow up to new levels of acceptance. I am trying to accept that, if it is about money, it is all right—as long as there is affection and sexual activity. My body is quite satisfactory actually. Having been a dancer finally pays off when you pass the 7-o.

And maybe I should be pulled up again a bit, although everyone says I look fine. Aged but fine. You never know what they really mean. I remember having lunch with Natasha and Charles in Paris when I first considered some surgery. When I announced I was considering going under the knife, Natasha said, "But, darling, you don't need it." Then, tilting her head judiciously while studying me, she said, "Well, the neck maybe." So French.

I was in my midsixties then. Fenil was perhaps twelve years old at that time. If I can even consider the possibility of this love affair I must be strong.

I invited Fenil to go up to Aguas Dulces with me and some French friends, Frans and Leonce. He was on his summer vacation and his pittance of a salary didn't allow him to go to the shore. He accepted. He has all the month of February as a holiday. February, of course, is mid-summer in Uruguay. It was approaching the end of the month, and he hadn't left the city. My motives were ambivalent. Truly. I really did want him to have the fun of a weekend at the beach. And I did want to spend some time with him to see who he was and if I was reading cues correctly or fantasizing.

I must say this: I suspect that Fenil has good taste. He dresses neatly and well on his little salary. He wears neat, tight little shirts with short sleeves in the evening, and for the beach, he has a pair of light blue shorts with a narrow white stripe around each leg. They are not inappropriately short. He has large thighs, and he is a bit self-conscious about this. As he walked down the beach ahead of me with Frans and Leonce, I could see that he has a long and well-muscled back. I like a nice back on a man. What did Mae West say? "He was a man and I like that in a person." That's me.

Somehow, Fenil makes me think of a small child I saw begging when I was up at Rivera on the Brazilian border for Mardi Gras last year. After the parade, we walked back to the car and were followed by a little boy who couldn't have been more than six. He had an adult haircut and was neatly dressed. As we spoke for a moment on a street corner before going to our separate cars, he waited quietly by the side of a nearby corner. It was clear what he wanted. Everyone else noticed but ignored him. I went over and gave him a fairly large bill. He looked at it, put it in his pocket, and then gave me a kind of two-fingered salute to his forehead as a thanks. It was a very adult gesture he had certainly seen somewhere. He walked away like a little man and I wondered how many brothers and sisters and perhaps incompetent parents he had to be helping. I hoped that he would grow up to be handsome and make enough money to help everyone in his family. I even think of going back to Rivera and looking for him. I have the same hopes for Fenil that I do for him. Poverty is really the most indecent thing in the world, and ignoring it is an indecent thing to do.

As we drove around the countryside near Aguas Dulces, Frans drove and Fenil and I sat in the backseat. He sits with his legs very widely spread, which I think is typically Latin American male. He leaned on me and I leaned on him. I have no way of knowing if that indicates intimacy or not. Perhaps in these countries men lean all over each other all the time.

At the end of the weekend we left Frans and Leonce in my house in Aguas Dulces and took a bus back to Montevideo. Our narrow bus seats pushed us into even more leaning upon each other. Whatever else he may be, Fenil has a very sweet temperament. There may be other aspects, which will surface later, of course.

On the bus trip he told me that he left his home in the country at fourteen to come to Montevideo. He did every kind of work from handing out leaflets in the streets to short-order cook, you name it. He also worked as a prostitute. I asked him where. He said on the main avenue and in a park that I often cross on the way to the Sunday antique market. He said, "What else was I to do?" He said he never had a problem having sex with women but sometimes with men he "just couldn't do anything."

"It's really nothing to apologize about," I said. He said he was glad to be able to stop doing it when he joined the police force and had a steady job. He said, "It made me grow up faster than a lot of other people," and I can easily believe that. He sees clearly that he is the only one among his two brothers and his parents who may move up out of the morass of the poor. And in doing so pull them up along with him.

Before I left Montevideo, his younger brother joined us for dinner. He is eighteen, works as a stock boy in a supermarket, and supposedly is a very talented soccer player. Fenil said he is under contract to a soccer team that is not going to go anywhere and needs his contract bought out. If that was a hint I ignored it.

We joined friends at the Fun-Fun Club, a tango-singing nightclub, after dinner. I don't think either Fenil or his brother had ever been in such an establishment before. Fenil sat next to me, and I suddenly felt a strong attachment for him and his manliness in dealing with what some could consider misfortunes. He had told me that afternoon that he had lived with a young woman for a time when he was eighteen and nineteen, and he has a two-year-old son who spends every other weekend with him. Later his younger brother made it very clear he had no plans to get himself in a similar situation. This is very likely a classic Uruguayan scenario. They have a 50 percent divorce rate.

Sitting next to Fenil I noticed that he has perfectly formed ears, and I felt a strong urge to put his ear into my mouth. Feeling that, I knew I was moving to a level that was quite different from just being attracted to a young "cute" guy. I really haven't felt that attraction for him before. But being less than two feet from him frequently in the past few days, something happened that was much more physical than visual.

When we spoke on the telephone a few days later, Fenil told me he had given his life savings, about one thousand dollars, to his brother to buy out his soccer contract so he could sign with a better team. I told him he could move into the guest room in my house, so he could save up another nest egg by not paying rent.

Mr. P.

Just so you don't think that I am some kind of hopeless old fart with a hopeless crush on some Latin American fifty years my junior, I want you to know I actually do have a kind of boyfriend who just arrived out of the blue in Paris.

Mr. P., Mr. Peter.

I had met Peter some time ago when he was writing music for a show a friend of mine had written and was producing. What do I remember about Peter? He was younger. Had dark hair. There was a sort of eager air about him. That was all.

Peter then moved to Germany. Although he was American he had been born there. He spoke fluent German. He had then been on television as a child in Italy and also spoke fluent Italian. All these things I learned later.

Peter called me and said he wanted to meet me in Paris. I never say no to anything unless I really can't do it. I was coming from Paris after being in London seeing another man I have been hanging around with for the past seven years or so. I was almost in love with this man and probably would have undergone one of those newfangled gay marriages with him if he had wanted to. Grant. Grant Radke. Shorter than I am but that wasn't it. Somehow it wasn't gelling. I was distracted by Fenil. And Peter's coming to Paris was very incidental.

I put him on the folding couch in the sitting room. We went to dinner with friends. I learned that he is extremely well educated. Knows a great deal about art and history and literature and often embarks all alone on a weekend just to visit some old town he has heard about. He is very sensitive to the atmosphere of old cities. I don't think I thought much about Peter and was surprised the last night he was visiting when he said, "Don't you feel all alone in that great big bed of yours? I could join you."

I explained that I was trying to sort out what was going on with Grant Radke and didn't like the idea of sleeping with one man when I was still involved with another one. Although "involved" would be pushing it a little bit when it came to Grant. Actually, I didn't find Peter sexually attractive.

Then the next morning as I passed through the sitting room en route to the bathroom, he was pulling on a T-shirt or pulling off his pajamas and I noticed his legs. Great. Great thighs. And I remembered that he was a fencer. And suddenly I found I *was* interested in Peter.

The downside of Peter is that he and I stand at opposite ends of the spectrum politically. He is very concerned about Communism. I explain that, except for Cuba, this political direction has pretty well faded. Mentally he seems to be somewhere in the late 1930s. The things he is very concerned about largely aren't very important in the chaotic world of international moneymaking that is churning around us right now.

I always find that when people are overly concerned with the affairs of the world they are not concerned enough about their own personal affairs. Peter is in his early forties. Because he was born in Germany, he has a German passport, a decent job, a decent income, but his dreams of working in theater aren't going much of anywhere. He likes me because I'm tall and blond and am not particularly intimidated by the world. I don't agree with Peter at all about his political views but don't argue with him. I have learned that much at least. When he starts on a rant, I just hold two fingers up in front of me in the sign of the cross, as though exorcizing a vampire, and he stops.

Anyway, the next time I went back to Paris, Grant Radke was history and Peter arrived from Germany, and we went to bed together and this has now been going on for a number of years. Three? Four? He likes the mountains. I like the shore. He likes eating meat. A lot of it. I don't want to eat anything I am not willing to kill. Which pretty much leaves fish. He is a very conservative dresser. I am always willing to try the new thing. He is very aware of the people around him in public. I am not, which leads him to say often, "Keep it down, will you?" And I respond, "I don't give a fuck. I don't know any of these people here." Which only disturbs him more. There you have it.

I am not in love with Peter, but we have intimacy. I don't think he feels what we call love. He excuses himself by claiming that he may have a touch of Asperger's syndrome. But he did say, "No one has ever paid this much attention to me." So that's what we have.

My feelings for Mr. P. are physical. He is easily affectionate, and I love being in bed with him, warm and touchable. I like being with him and his kind of quirky but unquestionable masculinity and his childlike love of nature. Intellectually, we are on different planets. He represents the great argument that our minds and our bodies have completely different programs. I love being with him. We agree on practically nothing.

Fenil, on the other hand, has that hard-driving, ram-it-to-you kind of Latin American sexuality, which is something completely different. Mr. P. is cuddly-fucky. Very nice.

My Injured Foot

The summer when I was twelve I cut my ankle very badly. Only this morning as I was awakening did I realize that it was the same year that my father died. He died the previous winter, just two days before my twelfth birthday. I don't need to go into how. We never got along.

It must have been early summer when I cut my foot. My mother was home. She had started teaching school once my father died and normally left the house before my sister and I did on school days. But this was Saturday.

I was lying on my bed reading, and my mother called me, for breakfast perhaps. I was lying sideways on the bed and decided for some smart-alecky reason to push myself off the bed using my feet against the wall. One foot went through a window. My badly gashed ankle gushed with blood as I called out for my mother. She bound it up with a towel, called the doctor, and helped me hobble out to the car.

Dr. Martha Goltz sewed the wound up, and I spent the rest of the summer on crutches, reading most days with my foot propped on a chair with a cushion under it. What was called "proud flesh" grew in the wound, and it has always been a sizeable scar, prompting questions from doctors whenever I've had a physical examination, of which there have been many through my years of school and the U.S. Navy and insurance applications.

I studied ballet and danced professionally on that damaged ankle and have always exercised almost daily without problems. But very recently extending my exercises into yoga and body stretching, my placement on my feet is changing, for the better, and I am aware of not standing squarely on my feet. And as I do, the injured ankle and its foot have become sore. And I am prompted to think of the original injury.

Did I at twelve, with my father recently dead and the prospect of beginning summer and part-time jobs and entering high school soon after and playing all the high school sports (which I subsequently did and hated), injure myself unconsciously but deliberately? The discipline I learned from my mother kept it from ever interfering with my progress through my teens. It never bothered me any more than did my homosexuality. My mother's and my grandparents' instillation of a sense of self-worth made it seem quite acceptable: "If it's me, it must be all right."

And now, in my seventies, the circle comes round. I am correcting the position of my body on the foot that was altered by that early injury. I injured myself perhaps to avoid the responsibilities I saw looming. But I accepted them anyway. And now I am returning to my pre-injury self. My great friend Jean Ann said to me years ago, "Some people look upon homosexuality as a sin. Some people look upon it as a crime. You seem to look upon it as a luxury." As I was brought up to think of myself as special, perhaps I have seen homosexuality as something special. Not exactly a luxury, but not for everyone. I have been lucky.

The Only Thing I've Ever Killed

This is a chapter I'd really rather not write. But I must. Because I always think I have no secrets and will tell anyone anything if they ask. And this is something I would tell you if you ask. But it's unlikely that you would think of it.

First, you should know that I am a good shot. I have no idea why. I am adept at only two sports: swimming and shooting. I don't think you can call dancing a sport.

I was probably under ten when I accompanied my older brother hunting in nearby woods with his BB gun. He killed a squirrel. I didn't like it at all. And saw no reason for it. The squirrel had done us no harm, and we certainly weren't going to eat it.

When I went to Naval Officer's School in Newport, Rhode Island, I had no trouble hitting the targets. And when I was a junior officer on the aircraft carrier, we had small arms drill, shooting at cans catapulted from the poop deck. Just lead with the gun; the bullet and the can will meet somehow. I could do that.

And when we sailed into Hong Kong bay to rescue General Claire Chennault's crappy and worn-out planes that were left from the commercial airline he had attempted to start in China, we were under the range of Communist guns and had to be prepared to repel boarders. All officers had to wear sidearms. Somehow, I knew I wasn't going to have to shoot a Communist and was reassured when I looked over the side and saw a launch from the British Embassy, full of officers in white shorts and ladies in pretty dresses with parasols. They had come to greet us. Communist guns were certainly not going to be part of the reception.

31

At dinner parties when some butch guy is discussing hunting, I say, "I could never kill an animal, but there are people I could shoot." There have only been two truly evil people I have known in my life, people who took pleasure in damaging other people's lives. I could have shot either one of them if I could have gotten away with it.

But I did kill an animal. Our family pet cocker spaniel, Silky. She was very old and liked to sleep in the driveway ruts that led from the garage to the street. I suppose the dust was cooler in the summer evenings. I must have been about nineteen. Home from college. Probably the summer I worked as a reporter for the local newspaper, published in a nearby small city.

I was home alone that evening, an unusual thing in itself. People I knew who were working at a summer resort on nearby Lake Michigan called me. Why didn't I come down to a party they were having?

This would be a first: driving alone through the night for ten miles or so to the lakeshore. A very adult thing to do. My mother was out for the evening with a man she was seeing in a very unromantic way. At least on her part. The family car was in the drive.

I ran out of the house, jumped into the car, and backed rapidly out of the drive. Right over the dog.

But worst, I heard the yelp, looked down from the window, and saw Silky, ears flapping, lying upside down right below the driver seat. I panicked and backed out further, running over her again. There was a definite bump, and the car passed over her body. Her body lay inert. Perhaps I could have saved her if I had simply gotten out of the car and pulled her out from under it. And the question I can never answer is, "Did I want to finish her off to avoid the nuisance of an injured dog?" No. I think in my panic I just wanted to get the car off her.

I looked around. There was a light on at the neighbors', the Lamberts. I ran over and went in. Jack Lambert, a year older than me, was reading in an armchair under a lamp. He was alone.

"I just ran over Silky," I told him.

He came out with me. We found an old piece of carpet in the garage, wrapped the dog in it, and dug a hole in the garden behind the garage to bury her. Once she was buried Jack returned to his book. He was always a silent, dependable type. Are there any of them left anywhere? I went in the house and went to bed on the sleeping porch. Not to sleep.

When my mother came home, as she crossed the porch after saying good night to Fred . . . no kisses . . . I sat up and said, "Mom, I ran over Silky and killed her." And burst into tears. She sat down on the bed and held me. Of all her children I think she found it easiest to be affectionate with me. I'm not physically standoffish. She calmed me down, and I'm sure told me that Silky was very old and it was time for her to go. But it definitely ended my childhood. Our sweet, loving cocker spaniel, so docile and gentle, that we had had for at least twelve years, was gone. And with her, some kind of sweetness and gentleness fled from my life, too.

And I think it stunted me. I have always disliked driving since. I always did dislike driving and never got over it, although I've driven a lot and am an excellent parallel parker. My mother was, too. She taught me.

But also it started a certain self-confidence. I have wandered all over the world, but never casually. I want things buttoned up, not left to chance. Whom else might I run over if things are left to chance?

The thing that strikes me, now that I am in that period where many of the people with whom I've shared my life are dying, is that I must go forward alone. Many friendships are the affinity one has for someone else who has crossed the great desert of life in the same wagon train and has survived. Someone like yourself who has survived the dangers of times like the 1960s, when many fell by the wayside from drugs and excess. And again in the 1980s, when AIDS swept so many away. And now in this new century, age is taking even those who have survived all this.

Of course, I have many younger friends who will survive me, but it's not the same. None of them remember Mary Quant. Or even before that when Eartha Kitt sang "Monotonous" in *New Faces of 1956*. And even before that, Ella Raines. Or Angela Lansbury when she was the villainess in *The Harvey Girls*. I've always had affection for obscure actresses, and she was that then. I even remember her when she sang "Good-Bye Little Yellow Bird" in *The Picture of Dorian Gray*. Hurd

Hatfield starred. He never starred again. Jane Greer. Evelyn Keyes. Gloria Grahame. They didn't have to be nice like the big stars. Lizabeth Scott. I loved that long, blonde side-part, held back with a diamond barrette. You knew she did it, whatever it was that was done. And now, even if you're out in public looking swell and having fun, dressed in silver lamé by Jean Paul Gaultier, you are still left alone with your memories.

What Can I Tell You
about Grant Radke?

I would have married Grant Radke. Of the men I have been involved with, which are not legion, he was the only one. And why? I think because he is so immersed in his business life you would never get his full attention, which is good. What doomed us was that I could never get enough attention.

I met Grant through friends at dinner. A good bit shorter than I am. Stocky. A good body. I don't think I would have paid him much attention except that on our way to dinner with the gay couple who introduced us, one of them said, "You're going to have dinner with us and Grant Radke." And the other one said, "Grant Radke. The dick of death." Well, that certainly gets your attention.

Grant is very good socially. A very good smile. Plenty of conversational topics. Asks you questions about yourself, which is quite rare. I am the questioner myself and am quite used to finishing an evening knowing everything about someone's mother, his siblings, where he went to school, how he likes his boss. You know. The whole drill. And he doesn't even know your last name. Grant wasn't like that. Isn't like that.

At the end of the evening, he said, "I'd like to see you again." I said, "I'm going to New York Saturday for a few days. I'll call you when I get back." He replied, "I can see you're going to break my heart." I was caught off guard. I said, "All right, I can have lunch tomorrow, Friday." Which we did.

At lunch, I learned he was in a relationship with another man that he had been with for seven years. He was renovating buildings in Miami

Beach, a very profitable thing to do. His father and mother had been divorced when he was young. He had been an excellent student, working his way through college as a bartender. That's where those social skills came from. Grant was sexy but not my kind of sexy. Maybe not dark enough. My lovers have gone from being tall, blond, and Adonis-like to shorter and darker. I told friends I am going to wind up with a pygmy. And there was his lover of seven years. I've never been "a little bit on the side" kind of person. Well, that's not entirely true. But it is certainly not my thing. Kind of desperate, which I would like to think I am not.

Grant wanted to see more of me. Maybe he was lonely. The boy-friend was in Denver and did not come to Miami Beach often, if at all.

We had dinner together. He tried to kiss me at one point on deliver-ing me home and I put him off. He wasn't a real contender.

I gave a big garden party one evening for some charitable reason, and he was there, chatting with my great friend Babs Rockefeller. She was related to the Rockefellers in some very distant way. Later she said to me, "He's very attractive but that kind of man is very hard to hang onto."

We never slept together. Somehow the optimum moment came and went. Sometimes when we were out he would drink very heavily and I would have to take him home. Not often. And I thought perhaps he wanted me to take advantage of him. But the boyfriend always loomed. I guess I felt if the boyfriend became history we could be lovers. I couldn't consider myself *fatale* enough that he would leave the boy-friend for me. I know, doesn't this all sound very silly coming from someone in their seventies, male or female?

This kind of went on. Grant went to Texas to work on more renova-tion projects. I was flying out at regular intervals to see him. We sort of acted like lovers, but we weren't. I was really interested in his life and in him but the electricity wasn't strong enough for me to push our relation-ship further. I'm such a girl.

Since I have known him, Grant has become a big deal. Hired to head up a company developed to renovate and redo, he has since created his own company, which has become international. He loves success, is a big risk-taker, has good luck, and the more success he has, the more he wants it. I see him very regularly. Those moments in Texas are past. I have seen some of the men he has had in his life since his long-term relationship ended, and for the most part it seems he is perfectly okay with someone who just holds still. He also told me that in his seven-year relationship, they only had sex a few times in their first weeks together and he did not have any sexual relations with anyone else during those years together. I believed him.

In his years with that lover, they were a kind of ideal gay couple in Denver. They had a big, well-furnished home in one of the most upscale suburbs of the city. They were involved with charity projects and mingled with the best upper set, as Cole Porter would have put it. They were the token gay couple. I think for Grant he was happy to play the role of part of an accepted gay couple in high society as long as he wasn't really sleeping with his partner. He wasn't really gay. It's guilt being played out in a very strange way.

Grant remains attached to me and is interested in how my sometime affair with Peter is developing. He knows nothing of Fenil at all. Except perhaps that he exists. Sometimes I have to overdo it to make sure I know where I stand in certain situations. Last year Grant wanted to take me on a trip. He can be generous and has always sent baskets of flowers and goodies on holidays and birthdays and such. I settled on a trip down through Italy from Venice through Florence to Rome, as he had never visited these cities. Venice rather held his attention. Florence less so. And as the trip went on, he was increasingly on the telephone and sending e-mails, which I think is acceptable as he has become a tycoon.

One evening in Florence, I had made reservations at a restaurant on the terrace of an ancient townhouse. As we approached on foot he said, "You go in and take the table. I have to make a call and will be right there." I ordered a drink. In half an hour I ordered dinner. An hour later I had finished my dinner and then he appeared from around the corner. "I hope you're not angry," he said.

"I would probably be angry if we had a relationship. But since we don't, I'm fine," I said.

I then spent a week with Peter touring the Romantic Road in Germany and decided to concentrate my energies on him. Somewhere underneath it all, Grant and I had had the potential for a deeply committed relationship. I could have stuck it out with him, but it just didn't happen. Perhaps I was aging ahead of schedule, too rapidly. Perhaps it was that "I'm not really gay if I'm not having sex in a relationship" thing of his. Peter also is sensitive about not having a gay public image, but he has some kind of need of me. And the whole thing with both men was largely motivated by my feeling, "I'm over seventy. I shouldn't really be rejecting these men."

When I was younger, I very likely would not have launched any kind of relationship with either of them. And I am still capable of having these strong feelings of wanting to have a relationship with some man. Because there is Fenil.

Old Songs

As I fixed some breakfast for myself this morning (toast and tea, that's all) and was singing some old song or other, I remembered that frequently people have said that I was singing what my subconscious was thinking. A few days ago, I had excavated "Be Careful, It's My Heart," a hit from the 1940s. I was driving north with the millionaire. A few days later, he mentioned that he didn't want to break my heart. I assured him that this was very unlikely, and he replied, "But you were singing about it." And perhaps he had something there.

My second brother was given to singing snatches of popular songs, as did my sister. And often I thought their songs indicated a state of mind. As far back as my college days when I briefly had a girlfriend to whom I was semi-engaged, she would pick up on this also. We were "pinned." I had given her my fraternity pin to wear. It was a ridiculous thing to do to a very nice girl I liked very much but certainly did not find sexually attractive. I was "pinned" to her because she was a Pi Phi sorority girl; it was a way of showing my fraternity brothers that I was their social superior. Anyway, she, too, would often say that the songs I sang revealed an inner state of mind. I pooh-poohed her, but of course she was right. The reason I contemplate this is that now deep into my seventies, I can accept that perhaps I am not exactly the person I think I am.

A recent visitor to my home in Uruguay, the high-flying Suzanne, reminded me that in the past I would sometimes appear at parties in Paris with her as my date as a kind of smoke screen to at least partially conceal or confuse my identity as a gay man. I wanted to contradict her but had to accept that she was right. I was not alone. Gay men of that period, the 1970s, would not have taken their male lover as their date to a party. Suzanne was not the only woman who would accompany me to advertising agency functions and the like. To this day, male film stars will go to the Academy Awards accompanied by their mother. Strange, isn't it, that the theater and motion picture industry would be one of the last bastions of "no gays" when it is fully accepted in the medical and legal professions, and even the government?

Suzanne's reminder made me feel ashamed of myself. One, for not taking a stronger stand on admitting my gayness. And two, my deceptiveness later in announcing that I had never been in the closet.

To look back on one's life and admit faults can't help but lower your self-esteem. Although I also allow myself the redemption that this was customary behavior at the time. Only the flaming queens with the fluttering wrists and imaginary bustles were very certainly gay in the eyes of others. And even they, if openly confronted with it, would dissemble and avoid answering.

So I must pay attention to the old songs that crop up in my day to read their messages to me. I can remember as early as the age of seven hearing my older brothers (Really? They were only three and five years older than me) playing records like "Deep Purple" and "Skylark" on a smallish half-size Victrola we had. A wind-up one. The songs of that prewar period were very pretty, even lovely, with very danceable melodies. It was the period of the Big Band. Everyone went dancing. A star of the motion pictures was Fred Astaire, a dancer. This would be unthinkable today. Does social dancing truly exist anymore? Isn't it just shrugging and shuffling to a heavy beat, never touching your partner? Except perhaps to press your buttocks into his crotch. Buttocks and crotches didn't exist in the 1930s. Just lovely flowing dresses and floating over the dance floor with a long, striding movement.

I think my entire concept of what love and relationships should be was formed by films and magazines of that prewar and wartime period. You would find fulfillment in the arms of some man who wanted you, and it probably wouldn't last. This was the war's effect. Everything was about love that was only for now. Songs like "How Little We Know,"

"I'll Get By," and "I Don't Get Around Much Anymore." There were hundreds of them about failed or missing love. Add to this that I never hankered for a domestic relationship. Cooking and housekeeping were not among my goals. Having some man crawl all over you was certainly among the pursued goals. Actually, it was very unlike today's modern homosexuals, who have an ideal goal of replicating their parents' lives. I certainly had no desire to copy my parents. Their life together as I had observed it consisted largely of bickering and worrying about money. Which was what most marriages seemed to be, as I saw them in the Depression. Their affection or caring about each other was rarely demonstrated, although I do remember coming upon them in the kitchen hugging and forcing my way between them as I hugged them also.

I wanted romance, and I have been very fortunate, having had my major romances extending over longish periods of time. I never expected men to be reliable or faithful. Only to be handsome and sexually exciting. Men can deliver that pretty consistently. The responsibility part you pretty much have to take care of yourself.

As a woman, I would have been much unhappier than I am as a gay man. In a gay relationship when the romance and sex part is over, you are out of there. As a woman, usually burdened with children even if you have a decent wage-earning career, it is not that simple. For me, having sex with someone when you don't feel like it is the worst. Yet many women must do it all the time. And being a prostitute? Forget the shame. Just think of the boredom and discomfort. All prostitutes must go straight to heaven. What a rotten way to earn a living.

When my sister told me she no longer felt like sleeping with her husband (she married a Tab Hunter lookalike who rapidly came to resemble Henry the Eighth), I told her, "Darling, you don't have to."

When I told my oldest brother he quickly said, "You shouldn't have told her that." I wonder what his wife would have added to that conversation. The idea of having sex with someone when you know he or she doesn't want to boggles the mind. That is really low.

My sister and I were close in age, resembled each other, and knew all the same songs. She married and stayed married, her life perhaps a continual exhibition of what mine might have been if I had been a woman.

She always said of her husband, "I might kill him, but I will never divorce him." I would have certainly killed him had I been married to him, and frequently told him so.

Sex Incidents

Fenil has a curious way of revealing things about his sex life, obviously for some reason, but a reason I find difficult to ascertain. Walking with him down Avenida 18 de Julio he told me again that he had worked as a teenage hustler and that the park on the avenue as you approach the university buildings was where he had picked up men and couples. He said he had to do it to earn money and that the men just gave him blowjobs and he had intercourse with the women at times. Perhaps he wanted me to know this because he had been off to Brazil with the friend from Miami who first introduced us and knew that he exchanged sex for favors.

Of course, he had told me about the Brazilian trip when I would have been ready to accept that the plump little friend of mine was interested in him but not making any sexual headway. He wants me to know these things. Which is a good thing. And can be a bad thing. Every time he tells me something more, it is something I have not anticipated. I certainly don't brood about what he's doing sexually or has done.

Walking down my street one evening going to my house, he told me that he had had a long relationship with an older man when he was eighteen and nineteen who had promised to take him to the United States. This is some American man in his sixties who may be a diplomat. Fenil was vague on that point. Finally, after some two years with the man postponing and postponing, it evidently became clear that he wasn't going to come through on getting Fenil to the United States. And he dropped the man. This was possibly to let me know he had already been through the drill of prospective emigration as a sexual lure. I can, of course, never get into that exchange of favors with Fenil.

43

Mainly because it is such a cliché. I don't mind tossing pride and self-respect out the window. I just don't want to have a life that's a kind of joke. It's so expected.

Just recently, I have seen a good bit of his handsome father, who is a mechanic in the Air Force. And his younger brother, who is cute, whereas Fenil and his father are handsome. Fenil told me that his brother also peddles his sexual favors. And in this conversation he told me that clients give his brother a blowjob, and then he fucks them. He said that he also had done this and that he thinks his brother likes to do it. That he had actually had intercourse with a male client was new. He said there is a steady bantering between the two of them as to how they suspect each other of actually liking sex with men.

Very recently he told me that after an evening of playing soccer his brother and he had gone back to his place and watched a porn film together. I told him I didn't think this was such a good idea as it might lead to sex play between the two brothers. And Fenil said, "Of course, we were both like this," making an upright gesture with his fist and forearm to imitate an erect penis. "You could hear the sound in the night, *hunk-ah, hunk-ah*, then 'Awwwwww,' and then the toilet paper cleaning up," he said. He made gestures of wiping a penis off with paper. Then he told me that recently his brother and he had taken a woman home and they had both had sex with her and that she had wanted more but they had had plenty.

He often talks about sex and has said that when he has sex with women he prefers that they leave immediately after sex, as he is no longer interested in them. I told him about my first great love affair and that after the first time we had sex we fell back into each other's arms and my lover said, "This must be love if we want to hold each other right after sex." I was making a kind of point that I don't think was made.

Meanwhile, Peter in Hamburg is sending me e-mails that very intellectually, yet poetically, make it clear that he would like to fall in love with me.

He has sent me his most recent movie script. I have to say Peter doesn't think small. His scripts are always about Columbus or Garibaldi or some subject that would require casts of thousands and many millions of dollars. No kitchen drama for Peter. The new script is a translation of something curious from the nineteenth century that he has modernized. I rather like to sleep with him because it is like sleeping with someone from the nineteenth century. He is pretty mad, Peter, but he does want to sleep with me, and as far as I know, no one else does.

As for Fenil, who knows if I am being manipulated, strung along, or what? But I plan to surprise him by absolutely not putting our relationship on any kind of sexual basis. Which is going to be a rather tough program when I put my arms around him and feel his strong back and his strong arms holding me close. Fenil has that effect on everyone, and he well knows it. There's that aura. And that bulging fly on his pants.

Writing

I think I just finished my twenty-first book. For some reason, I can never keep it quite straight in my head. And by finished, I mean published. I don't really count a book unless you can go into a store and buy it. I have four novels and a how-to book written and ready to be published, so I guess I actually have finished twenty-five books.

This flood only began some fifteen years ago, and I have had one or two books published every year since. As I tell everyone, you can never be said to have ruined your life after seventy, and I feel I should write and produce the books I have because I don't think anyone else is going to.

I love the twenty-first century, and I think my writing and books have perhaps been pushing toward a kind of unhampered thinking I see in younger people. The male nude books I have done were to make public all the photographs that were hidden away or traded among homosexuals and to generate some feeling of casualness about the subject. I think women's liberation has aided a lot, as men have become the sex objects women once were.

It seems to me, too, that American men are, for the most part, uncomfortable with sex. They don't wallow in it and want it to last. I think they want to get it over with and get back to the television. Homosexuals are the ones who have been left to really enjoy, read about, discuss, and involve themselves deeply in sex. Perhaps I am wrong, as there is a major business going on with heterosexual videos. But again, this is observing, not partaking.

My books sell, particularly the photo collections. But it is the novels that make me feel that I am actually productive and using myself to create. And although they are not really autobiographical, they do draw upon life experience. I wonder if other writers find as I do that once they use life experience in their writing, it disappears from their memory. If I should reread parts of a novel several years later, I find I have completely forgotten the details I recount there. It is as though you are shedding your past once you turn it into a story.

For me, it helps me make sense of my life. It wasn't just lived for me alone. If it can be shared with others, then there is some reason for it. And why is it we feel it should make some sense?

I think a lot of literature contains characters that may be original and fascinating and theatrical but actually don't have many of the qualities we know from ourselves and our relationships with others. I try to be honest in my books and not have people feel or say things I don't think people would really do. I want everyone to be a real person, not some stick figure that suddenly appears to keep the plot moving.

And the same thing with events. Even in very highly regarded novels, I find the author has stuck in some "by chance" event that is essential to plot but not very likely or completely unlikely in reality. That kills the book for me. I feel that I am now reading something that is not designed for me to learn from but only to amuse me. And I do not wish to be amused with no end result.

Knowing this, I hope I will be able to write until the end of my life. Because when I write, I feel I have done something. To this point, I have rarely spent a day just passing time. And when I look at my peers, that seems to be largely all that they do. I want to go to the end involved with other people. Hopefully, even having sex with them. I have a horror of being someone other people feel they should pay attention to or of whom they should take care. That reversion to a childlike state is always a bore for other people.

So, I will continue writing and I hope have something of interest to say and recount. Few have ventured from eighty to ninety and written about it, so perhaps I can cross that particular desert and bring back some news.

The Little Tree

When I was twenty-eight I went through a bad patch when I couldn't find any reason to go on living. I had thrown a career in advertising or publishing into the toilet and became a dancer. And now it was very clear that I would never become a star, and if you didn't become a star your career was going to be over by thirty anyway. All those young, bouncy boys coming up behind you were so much more hirable.

I had also been through great disenchantment with my second major lover, who had come to fulfill the lyrics of that famous barroom song, "He may be good fucking, but he's no fucking good." I had lost my way in the water, living in my dreary little cold-water flat in Chelsea in New York, doing temporary work computing research data in those pre-computer days. I couldn't see where to go next. I'd done everything I had ever really wanted to do and had come to a dead end. It wasn't so much that I was suicidal. It was more that I was already dead. I know it sounds melodramatic, but you forget your own life between twenty and thirty. At twenty-eight, it becomes quite clear that you are not simply living the same year over and over again, but that the years are passing. Relentlessly, you are being carried forward. But toward what? And for what reason? Because I am a high-energy person, I had already pretty much worked my way through my own plans for myself. There was nothing more to want.

And then one afternoon in this mood, I came down the steps from the tenement building where I lived on Sixteenth Street near Eighth Avenue, past the railings and cement steps, turned to the right, and as I walked toward Seventh Avenue, I saw a small tree, its green leaves newly emerged, standing in a wash of sunlight that fell between tired city buildings, bright against a red brick wall. And I understood something. That little tree didn't have a reason to live. It was living because it was alive. And that was reason enough. And it has been reason enough for me.

My Life in New York

Being in my seventies is a new experience for me. I wonder what it's like for other people. No one ever writes about it. I think people begin to live in their own past. I don't. The life I am living now is as interesting, perhaps more so, than any other period of my life. My body hasn't slowed down, not really, and I have never been one to sit around and be entertained. Frequently when I am watching a film, I say to myself, *What am I doing here? My own life is more interesting than this movie.*

There was a bar in Greenwich Village near where I lived called Chumley's. It had a kind of turnstile up-and-down staircase right inside the door, no sign on the door, and a handy backdoor through a courtyard to another street. It had obviously been a speakeasy during Prohibition. Mrs. Chumley, a tiny, red-haired lady, sat drunkenly at a corner table, a handkerchief folded neatly at her left. She spoke without making any sound, and when you had a drink with her, her lips would move, but there was no sound. Once I was by her side and I thought I actually could hear a voice. I leaned in very closely, and she was saying in a tiny, dying, lost voice, "I have a terrific sense of humor."

I remember coming out of my Grove Street apartment on a Saturday morning on my way to the Laundromat and thinking, *I am exactly where I want to be.* That's a good feeling. As for my sex life, I was seeing my great love from the ballet period of my life regularly. We were not truly lovers. Surely he was sleeping with lots of other men, too. But we met every couple of weeks, and that was fulfillment enough for me.

At work, there was a game where you used the number of times you had sex weekly, multiplied, divided, etc., and then the person administering this mystery test could tell you what your sex regularity was. When mine came out "every two weeks," the tall red-haired account executive who was doing the inquiry said to me, "You're probably the only one who isn't lying."

I saw many of my friends lowering their standards or slipping off into more and more casual sex, and I felt lucky that my work, ignoble though it may have been, was entirely engrossing and forced me to grow and comprehend.

Some years ago, I had an insurance agent for my house in New York who was of that Italian heritage of tall, husky men with wavy, light brown hair, and that kind of angelic-rounded face with large brown eyes you see in Renaissance paintings. That was Vincent Caligostro. He was quite a honey, Vincent, and married. I never asked if he had children. Though I never slept with him, he added to my sexual experience. He used to come to performances of mine from time to time with a gay friend—a young man of rather nondescript appearance whose face I can no longer conjure up.

Vincent was at my house one day selling me insurance and I said, "Vincent, let's talk some turkey. You let those young gay men, you know, give you blowjobs, don't you?" I could easily imagine it. Vincent sprawled back in someone's easy chair with his trousers undone. He admitted that he did and enjoyed it very much, as it was quite different from sexual intercourse with a woman. He said, "I think it takes another man to give a really good blowjob because women don't have a penis. They don't know what feels good where."

I said, "Well, one of these days you'll have to let some guy sit on it. You don't have to get undressed. It will be quite a different experience for you to be deep in some man's body when you come. And you don't have to move. Evidently, if you don't move you don't think you are cheating on your wife, so you might as well experience being in someone, too." He did, I learned later. And then moved on to actually taking his clothes off. And, adventuresome soul that he was, decided another man could actually enter him and he wouldn't have to move there either. Then, of course, he couldn't keep on the "nonmovement" track forever and wound up socking it to other guys as only Italian men can. And left his wife and became a kind of legend around Greenwich Village. I always liked to think of him as "The Unmovable Vincent Caligostro."

It was during this time that I interrupted my advertising career for a few years to manage a ballet school and its budding company. I met the man I always refer to as "The Love of My Life" at that time, and we, what can I say, got involved with each other for ten years. He was the great fulfillment for me. The kind of lover you can fall on the floor with on entering your apartment and tear each other's clothes off. The kind of lover with whom you can wake up the next morning and find your pajamas in little torn bits all over the bedroom floor. You don't really need another great lover after one like that.

At the end of ten years, I realized I either had to go crazy with him or leave him. I didn't really want to spend the rest of my life as a crazy person, so I bid him adieu. We still talk. I paid his rent for many years and eventually bought the house he lives in. That's the least you can do for your own past, I think. You can't abandon it. That's like pretending it never happened.

At this same time, my best friend was Armand, who was moving into a sexual world I might have entered too, but didn't. When Armand lived in New York, from time to time, he would get a call in the night from some young married man with whom he happened to work. And "happened" was the word. He never knew them well. They were not friends.

They would always be drunk, and their reason for calling was always the same, too. They had had an argument with their wife, or she had left, or there had been an angry phone call, something of that kind. And they had nowhere to stay. Was Armand's couch available? It was. And they would arrive, take a shower, and drop naked into Armand's bed.

Armand liked to sit on their upturned bodies, letting them plug in and out of him while he watched their slim, un-gym-trained bodies surge and recede.

He loved to see their faces twisted in that expression so like torture that curiously is the same expression of approaching ecstasy. And then watch their faces soothed and smoothed as they fell away from him. They rarely kissed while making love and never afterward. And he never

ever saw them again. Sleeping with him and quitting their jobs seemed to be related somehow.

And now, somehow, when I think of Fenil, he's one of those men who could be my fourth and last lover, to fill the last corner of the squared-off pattern of my life, but will not be. Very much like someone I knew toward the end of my advertising career in New York before I moved to Paris to continue it. Mischa. Handsome, dark, glittering-eyed, curly-haired Mischa. He was Romanian.

I knew him between his second and third marriages. Not for long. I had that same feeling for him that I do for Fenil. That feeling that inner barriers are opening, and I can give myself to this person completely. I have only felt it a few times before. And I think never with the man I spent thirty years with in bed and out. Our relationship was something else.

We almost slept together, Mischa and I, one wet night when we had had dinner and I was going back to his apartment with him. He lived in a small apartment in what had been a townhouse on the Upper East Side. In the outer entryway a young woman was waiting. She was someone Mischa knew who explained she was homeless now and wanted to stay overnight with him. She was more than homeless. She was part of a drug-heavy floating world of young people he moved in. Which I knew about and ignored. Her presence cut the cord that was holding Mischa and me together, and it never was connected again.

Somehow I believe these people are messengers, sent from somewhere to interrupt a pattern so that I am unable to go there. I used to be irritated by these interruptions. Now I accept them as some kind of gesture indicating that I am not to go in this direction.

I hadn't thought of Mischa for a long time, until recently when I was in New York. I happened to be stopping at Grey Advertising, where I had worked for so many years. I saw a man in an elevator that day. He had been a famous photographer once. Now he looked like his own replica in gray ashes, about to be blown away in the wind. That strange pearly gray color of skin and hair and eyes drug addicts get. I hate that man. He was living with the daughter of a movie director when I knew him in the 1960s. I knew him professionally. I never met her. I have always thought they were responsible for involving Mischa with drugs. I hate her, too, and I've never even met her. She had a momentary flurry as a model because of her father in those days. It was already over when she was with the photographer.

Mischa started doing a lot of drugs hanging out with them. The man I loved, Mischa, died at thirty. He had already been married three times and fathered two children. He had done a lot of drugs by that time, too. He died of cancer of the lungs. There may have been no connection but please don't tell me that. He had been a dark flashing beauty who went up in smoke.

These elevators had been up and down many times since Mischa had gone up in smoke, as the photographer would one day. Mischa and I must have stood side by side in this very elevator more than once. We had worked together at Grey. That's how we met. How could these elevators still be here? How could this building still be standing from the force that tore my heart out? The same force with which I hate that couple. I can imagine those lazy afternoons with Mischa hanging around in their Village apartment. Maybe there was sex. Mischa had a beautiful body.

The slippery glide from marijuana to cocaine to shooting up with heroin. Not nice. I don't find it hard at all to imagine the hurricane force of rage that whipped through Phaedra when she killed her two children and threw them at Jason's feet. That is what I have always felt toward those two silly people. And they never knew I even existed. I wonder if there is anyone out there who hates me the same way and whose existence I know nothing of.

Mischa was swept out of my life. And I stand prepared that Fenil will be, too. Although in a completely different way. I think Fenil will be swept off into bourgeois, middle-class heterosexual living. And I think it will suit him fine.

My Credo

When I am with someone, I belong to him. I don't even find other men attractive. Not as long as my man is sleeping with me. I lock in on that one man. Whether he cheats on me is immaterial. That may be his grasp on our relationship. It's not mine.

Sometimes when my knowledge of his infidelities becomes too overwhelming, I have slept with someone else, just so when I am with my lover I can tell myself, "I know we both have our little secrets." But there would never be any possibility of my leaving him for that other man.

And then, usually after some years of casual neglect, I will get up one morning and I won't be in love anymore. And I depart. There is never any possibility of reconciliation. I don't want to get into bed with someone to make "bamboola" as a rule unless I'm in love with him. There are any number of people who don't like me. And I have always said, "I'm not for everyone."

The Story
That Comes to You

The following poem came to me complete in the night except for the second line, which I improvised:

The Whore's Song
I'm forty-two years old.
Can't you tell?
I have a fur coat and rough edges.
Go to hell.

Today, while re-hanging the hammock in the garden, I had a strong flash of once having dreamed doing it. Are there layers of life going on that we are slipping back and forward to? There is a Chinese quotation about the man dreaming of being a butterfly. Or was he a butterfly dreaming of being a man? I am quite tired these days from over-entertaining. Fatigue either causes these thoughts or reveals them.

Here is a short story that also came to me in a dream, and I think you should read it. I think when these stories come to you in these intact ways, they are a kind of parable about you. Perhaps not a parable with a neat conclusion one can express in a clear-cut sentence. The general mood of this story about Mrs. Parry may be about a kind of atmosphere you may live in one day. Or a kind of atmosphere that others are living in, although their exterior life may be much more chockablock with things and activities than Mrs. Parry's world. Or, yet again, perhaps Mrs. Parry is telling me about a way to live.

Mrs. Parry

"Mrs. Parry isn't here," the woman said. Behind her I could see unpainted gray-weathered buildings straggling away across the dunes. They were encircled with a high fence of wooden slats and wire, the kind used to keep sand from drifting and beaches from eroding. It was bleached gray also. As were the hair and features of the woman standing at the long board gate.

"But she must be here. Her daughter said she sends monthly payments to this address." I pointed to the address on the gate. It was 25 Dune Road. A long, sandy pair of tracks ran across the dunes. My car had navigated it without too much difficulty. There hadn't been any indication of the twenty-four preceding residences on Dune Road.

"Are you her daughter?" the woman asked.

"I think you can see rather easily that I'm a man," I said.

"Humph. You can't tell anything these days with all these operations and everything," she said.

"That's awfully modern of you," I said. "Sorry. I'm a real authentic man, and my name is Mark Lamos."

"Are you family?" she said.

"No. Just a very good friend. I've come a long way to see her." I couldn't tell if this belligerent woman was really being hostile and insulting or if she was a resident here in some kind of seaside mental institution.

"Only family are allowed to see residents."

"But surely that can't be true. You're very isolated here. Your 'residents' must welcome guests."

"Nope, they don't," she said.

"I'm afraid I'll have to insist on speaking to the supervisor here."

"I am the supervisor."

"Well, I'm sure Mrs. Parry's daughter is going to want to come and take her mother to some other residence if she's not allowed to see old friends. Are you going to want that to happen?"

"Are you some kind of wise guy?"

"No. I'm from Boston. I've driven a long way. I've come across on the boat, and I don't fancy going back to Boston and telling Mrs. Parry's daughter I wasn't allowed to see her mother."

"Come," she said abruptly. "You can talk to the office."

Inside the fence there were no sidewalks or paths. Just footprints in the sand from building to building. No one was in evidence. I could see perhaps a half-dozen buildings, most of them resembling old one-room schoolhouses that had been dragged here and put down with no plan or organization. The office was one of the buildings. The gray-haired woman opened the door and let me in, closing the door behind me.

A short, fattish, youngish woman sat behind what seemed to be a red marble counter. Red and black. I couldn't tell if it was real or faux marble, painted. I touched it; it was real. The woman had what looked like very recent sunburn, and her hair fell tangled and dank around her face. She looked as though she had recently emerged from the sea on a hot day. Which was not at all the case on Martha's Vineyard. "I've come to see Mrs. Parry," I said.

It was hard to tell the woman's age. She could have been weather-beaten in her late thirties, or a fairly well-preserved woman in her sixties. "I don't know if we have anyone who can take you to see her right now," she said.

"Is she far away?" I said.

"Not far. But we don't allow visitors to walk about on the grounds unescorted."

I thought "grounds" was a fairly extravagant word for the sand and the saw grass that surrounded the clutch of gray shacks that made up this retirement home.

"What do you think, Fred?" She turned to a man who emerged from the room behind. He was tucking something into his pants and it wasn't his shirt. He didn't have a shirt on. His body was lean and good-looking below his wolfish face. Perhaps it was the long teeth and a smile that wasn't really a smile.

He seemed to be perspiring, and then I noticed what seemed to be a pizza oven on the wall where I had entered. The woman behind the counter seemed to be perspiring slightly, too. And then I saw that the room was painted red. A dark red, ceiling, walls, and floor. An unusual decor, I thought, for these people, who all seemed to be recently sunburned, red skins. Perspiring bodies. Wolfish smiles. A little hellish, perhaps?

The lady behind the counter agreed that since he . . . what did she call him? Her "colleague." That was it. Since her colleague was there she could accompany me to see Mrs. Parry.

We walked among the dunes and the weathered gray houses where there seemed to be no activity. Were there retirees in those faded, almost ruined buildings? There were more buildings than I realized, and I also noticed what had to be outhouses. Small buildings, some even with the traditional crescent moon cut in the doors. Mrs. Parry seemed to be in one of the more distant buildings.

My guide rapped on the door, as flimsy and weathered as the rest of the house. A woman opened it. It was Mrs. Parry, although I hardly recognized her. She had an old torn bathrobe wrapped around her and her gray hair hung tousled and stringy about her face. She had always been very well groomed, tidily dressed with her hair center-parted, waves reaching back to a chignon. This crone's feet were stuffed into worn rabbit-skin slippers I could never have imagined Mrs. Parry owning, but here she was.

"Mrs. Parry? It's Mark. Mark Lamos." She didn't seem to be at all fuzzy. "Mark," she said, "imagine you coming all the way out here to see me. Come in. Come in. Not you, Pauline. I'm fine. I can walk my friend back to the office." My guide fell back from the step where she had begun preceding me into the house. Shack. Shed. Whatever it was.

It was dim in the building. I saw several other old ladies lying and sitting on crudely built bunks along the walls. "This reminds me of—" I didn't finish my sentence.

"A concentration camp." Mrs. Parry finished my sentence for me. "Sit down." She gestured toward a bunk whose blankets were neatly pulled up and tucked into place. We sat.

Light filtered in from some windows high up under the eaves. This had perhaps been a corncrib or a pigsty at one time. "Are you all right here, Mrs. Parry?" I asked.

"Perfectly," she said, arranging her bathrobe about her and pushing her hair back from her face.

"What do you do here?" I said.

"Nothing," she said. "I like it that way."

"Where do you eat?"

"They bring us pizza. Actually, quite good pizza."

"That's all? No vegetables? Nothing else?" I said.

"Pizza is quite a complete food. Tomatoes, cheese, sausage, anchovies. It's all there. And Coca-Cola. Coca-Cola of the diet variety. Although I hardly need to diet. But we're avoiding the sugar. Some of the people here have dietary problems."

"I must have seen the pizza man on my way through."

Mrs. Parry said, "Sexy, isn't he? He's new." I didn't know quite where to go next with our conversation. Mrs. Parry had become quite colloquial. When I knew her in Boston, she would have never referred to anyone as "sexy." "Attractive," perhaps. A pizza man was definitely not someone who would have been described as "attractive." Was this woman really Mrs. Parry?

I said, "He seemed to have sunburn."

"He just arrived recently. They all come and go at a great rate. Only we, the guests, seem to stay on forever and forever. Life seems to go on endlessly here. Or perhaps it just seems endless. But that's good at my age. I suppose the workers, who are younger, get bored because there is nothing to do out here at the end of this lane in the sand."

Mrs. Parry seemed to be getting a good bit more poetic than I ever remembered her being.

"Are you really all right here, here at the end of a lane in the sand? What does Muriel think of this?" I gestured about me.

"Oh, Muriel has never seen this. Only brochures. And the brochures aren't of this place. They're of Sandy Harbor, a guest . . . what would you call it . . . compound . . . you pass on your way out here. No, Mrs. Sanford has done something quite unusual here, I think. She has created a retirement community that suits retirees just fine.

"When you go into a retirement home, everyone assumes you desire to go on living as you always have to the nearest degree possible but that's not true. Everyone is bored to death with the way they have been living by the time they are in their seventies. Perhaps not everyone. Perhaps not Marlene Dietrich. But for the most part, if you are a drained remnant of the bourgeoisie you have had enough of upper-middle-class living. Bored to death is a good expression. Most people, if their health holds up, are finally bored to death.

"Mrs. Sanford realized this so she created a place with just the basics where no one has to keep up any kind of front any more. We just sit and listen to the waves and slide off into a state where we are practically dead already. When death comes, we scarcely know it. Sometimes I'm not even sure that I'm not dead already. You're not dead and coming for a visit here in heaven, are you?" She reached over and touched my arm and laughed.

It was quite clear that Mrs. Parry knew she was still alive and not just putting a good front on things. I said, "You're not just putting a good front on things?"

"No. No, not at all. I like being here. Perhaps 'like' is too strong a word. I prefer being here to being with Muriel or in some dreadful Boston home with all those stiff old folks. There they are really trying to put a good front on things.

"Old people don't explain themselves very well. Once you stop being concerned with what other people think of you, you begin to biodegrade. You remember your life quite clearly, but you don't really care. And you don't really care about people about whom you know very little, although you may have spent your life with them. Muriel, my niece, for example. I have no idea whom she is sleeping with. Or if she has ever slept with anyone. Or if she is a lesbian. Or is afraid of sex. We have never discussed any of these things. Only the weather, theater, literature, art, music, clothes. Speaking of what is truly happening in other people's lives is considered bad taste. So once you cross the barrier, as I have, there's really nothing left to say.

"For myself, the idea of living to be two hundred and still listening to Mozart, liking Impressionism, being interested in Arthur Miller, what horror! And *Romeo and Juliet*. By the time I was sixty, I could no longer bear yet another version, on ice skates, sung, danced, all black cast, nothing. No, some things wear out. And finally life wears out on you if nobody is doing great things anymore. Great music seems to have been created and pretty well finished in the nineteenth century. Great theater? I'll give you from Shakespeare to halfway through the twentieth century. Great painting? I think even Picasso is something of a farce. Modern art only means something to a handful of people. Film? Is it even an art?

"Perhaps I myself have just worn out as a perceptive vehicle for life. If so, then I must go, my darling. And I'm perfectly satisfied to spend my days in a torn bathrobe and unwashed hair, wearing slippers from God knows where."

"They don't wash your hair?" I said.

"I don't wash my hair. They don't do anything, other than give us clean sheets from time to time, toilet paper, and pizza. Mrs. Sanford has figured out quite a racket here. I'm proud of her."

"No wonder she doesn't want visitors," I said.

"None of us wants visitors." She reached over again to touch my hand. "Not that I don't enjoy seeing you. I always had a place in my heart for you, Mark, because you didn't want a place in the world I lived in."

"There was no place for me. I'm homosexual, and there would only be a place for me if I lied. And I didn't want to lie," I said.

"Well, isn't that the good part? If you hadn't been a homosexual you would have been just like me. Marking time throughout your whole life so it would look good to a bunch of people who finally care nothing about you at all. Because you care about me, you made the effort to come here to the end of the known world to see me." She patted my hand again.

"This is the end of the known world, isn't it?" I said.

"Oh, very much so. But I'm sure you came here for some other reason than just to see me. What is it? Because you must go soon, Mark. I have to go take a whiz, as Mrs. Sanford puts it so delicately."

"Was Mr. Parry gay? Homosexual?" I said.

"I know what the word 'gay' means," she said. "I wonder if Albert was what you'd call gay. He was never very enthusiastic about sex with me. Dutiful. Is there anything worse than having sex when you don't feel like it? If you do, you certainly go straight to heaven. Like that!" She made an upward gesture with both hands in an attitude of prayer. She went on.

"Do you think he slipped around and sucked on other people's private parts? In dark places? I hope not. I would never have minded him having an all-out romance. All clothes off. Spread out on a bed. Lights on. Or sunlight pouring through a window. He had a very decent penis. And a nice body. Somehow I don't think he would ever have had the nerve. But there you have it. He was someone I was married to for almost forty years, and that was a subject we could never have discussed.

"Fortunately for me, I had several other lovers so I got to know something about sex and love from other sources. I don't think it's reasonable if you really love someone to think they should limit their sexual knowledge to only you. Of course, if you're really imaginative and you like sex, you can hang onto a man's attention for a very long time. So few people are really any good at all at sex. I imagine you are." She looked at me.

I laughed. "I've never had any complaints," I said. "And it's true. You really can't demand that your lover only sleep with you. As long as he's sleeping with you enough. Of course, extracurricular lovers can be a threat to your domestic life."

"Your domestic life and your love life never have anything to do with each other," Mrs. Parry said. "Even if the same two people are sharing them. The person you share your love life with might be completely impossible for domestic living. I never liked domestic living that much anyway. I hate to cook. I'm not wild about cleaning either. Only ironing. I always liked to iron. When you are done, you clearly see that you have accomplished something. Unlike most activities.

"One man I loved very much was my husband's college roommate. Long after they were in college together. He really liked sex. But was quite stupid. And then a man quite a lot younger than myself who came to repair the refrigerator. Isn't that ridiculous? I really was crazy about Ronald. We were both married and had no intention of doing anything about it. You know you have thoroughly lived a sexual exploration with someone when you can let them go. At any rate, enough about me. Did I answer your question?" She stood up and straightened her bathrobe.

The woman on the next bunk said, "That was great, Isabel. I didn't know you had it in you. And I couldn't have said it better myself." Mrs. Parry did a little curtsy in her direction and moved toward the door. She went down the several steps with me.

"I can find my way back to the gate," I said.

"You're going to have to. I must dash over there." She gestured around the side of the building. The wind had picked up. Gray clouds were scudding overhead and seagulls were hanging under them, floating in the steady breeze. There was no sun.

"Your husband probably just dreamed about being gay, then," I said.

"Yes. I would imagine that is right." She turned to look at the sea. "I love it here. I am constantly reassured that although the waves are forever changing, the water that is breaking there is always the same. Nothing really changes. The idea that we're going somewhere is false." She hugged me and disappeared around the building, her gray hair wild in the wind, bathrobe hem flapping.

I found my way back easily through the dunes. There was no one at the gate, which was slightly ajar. I drove away.

Paris

I think I have left Paris definitively.
I sold my apartment and brought a few things to Miami Beach. So it
isn't entirely over. And I still have a country house in the Loire Valley.
But I first went to Paris almost fifty years ago, and although Paris hasn't
changed very much, I have. Do you think that sometimes we have lived
too much? It doesn't make me want to stop living, but just to stop living
in the same place. That's why I don't miss New York, where every corner
reminds you of someone you loved, somewhere you lived, somewhere
your aunt lived, and so on. All so many years ago.

And now Paris has become that for me. Paris had magic for me, but
in retrospect, you have to admit to yourself you never had a truly good
French friend. They never want to know you well enough that you
might call in the night when in need of help. Or want to borrow money,
the most horrifying thing a French person can imagine. No, your
friends are always of Russian origin in the previous generation or a mix
of nationalities. The French are there, cool and amusing and well
dressed, but never intimate.

It's strange, but a Frenchman I knew in New York when he was very
young and in whom I could have been interested is now calling me
and reminiscing and feeling affectionate. After a number of marriages
and presently wed he is wondering if the crossing of our paths was an
opportunity missed. Does it take a lifetime to work your way through
to what you really want, when it is far too late?

I think Peter rescued me from Paris. He and I came together there.
We have traveled together a lot. He has lived with me in Miami Beach.
He has lived with me in Montevideo. Although we are not lovers, we

are intimates, and it doesn't depend on where we are. He has lived all over the world, as I have. My relationship with him doesn't depend on a place. I had imagined that my relationship with Fenil would not depend upon a place, but now I feel it probably does.

Men and Cats

I have learned a number of things about men in their treatment of cats. Not that I am one of the "cat people" or a "dog person." Not at all.

One of my lovers gave me a cat in the early 1970s. A kitten from his household. I called the cat Gideon. Soon after, I found another grown cat with a collar in the streets of Greenwich Village. I called the number on his collar tag and found he had belonged to a diner that had burned. The owners departed and left Pierre, as I called him, behind. My sister visited me at about that time and said, "I didn't know you were that interested in pets."

I said, "I'm not. But now that I have them, I feel responsible for them."

"That's how I feel about the children," she replied. We are Michigan people. Not all that demonstrative and able to speak of it.

Another lover in the next romantic wave told me that he had had a cat that jumped from a second-story porch when he lived in Toronto. And then after being absent for some time, wandered back. He was living there with his wife. Spare me your criticism. I knew him before he was married. I will sleep with a married man if he was a lover before he was married. I'm not that uptight about adultery if the adultery is the lover's problem, not mine.

This has been a recurring pattern in my life. Men who fall half in love with me, then marry a woman, then wander back in a kind of half-assed way. None have ever managed to reach any kind of epic-level relationship with me. Their own indecision, I suppose.

Anyway, this man told me that when the cat leaped off the porch a second time and then wandered back, his wife and he heard the cat crying at the front door and refused to open it. His wife was French. French-Canadian. I can just see her pursed-up little mouth saying, "Non, non, non." And him obeying.

The cat finally wandered away. To find a better home, I can only hope. Perhaps there are some kindhearted people in Toronto. More kindhearted than my dithering boyfriend, who sealed his fate with me when he told me this story. I could imagine myself crying for admittance at the doorway to his heart. If you can't learn from a story like that, you'll never learn, and you deserve all the unhappiness you will get with that person.

Another friend, not a boyfriend, showed me a photo of himself playing with his cat when he lived in San Francisco. Then he told me he had taken the cat to the veterinarian and had him put down because he had been a feral kitten and attacked him around the house. I have chosen to believe that this was true. But I wonder if I would have found the cat's attacks too much to handle. If you can turn your affection on and off like that, where does love fit into any of this?

And now I have a new kitten in my already pet-congested home. When my sister and brother died, I inherited their pets. Two cats from her. A dog and a cat from my brother. I already had a dog and a cat: a dog that had been deposited on Lincoln Road in Miami Beach and left to find a home, and a cat that wandered out of a wheat field in France as a kitten.

The new kitten had evidently had a home and was deposited on the street in front of a friend's apartment building here in Miami Beach, complete with carrying case and food supply. I said, when my friend called, "You can't go to heaven once you've done something like that." So the kitten was put in my guest room (I was out of town), and instead of finding him a home on my return, I kept him. I call him Buster. His real name is Zebulon Pike. I think cats should have a real name that's not used. I got that from E. E. Cummings. I know, I know. My dog Bibi's real name is Vanessa. Go figure. We almost never say it. I am beginning to sound like an animal person, aren't I? At any rate, you can treat a lover shabbily. He has the resources to survive. Not a kitten.

And now, Buster has disappeared while I was in South America. Buster took to accompanying the pet sitters when they walked the dogs in the evening. And one evening, Buster just didn't return. I wonder if he is living handily in a nearby house here on Rivo Alto Island. I wonder if the pet sitters told me the truth about his disappearance.

My Little Conversation
with God

I've always felt that left to them-
selves people would finally grow up and do the right thing. But now
after seventy years and more of hanging around, I'm beginning to have
my doubts. I said to God, "They're beginning to look awfully programmed to me. Women just have to have babies no matter what. Men
just have to fight and be waited on."

"I know," God said. "You're not the only one to be disappointed.
They do seem to be awfully stupid. I have to keep reminding myself
that they used to be fish."

"They all do stuff that is so obviously not in their own best interests,"
I said. "But somehow they just can't stop themselves."

"It's difficult to explain. I guess love is the best example. You fall
in love with someone who's all wrong. Someone of your own sex, for
example, which is so hard for other people to understand. I don't even
quite get it myself, but 'Kismet,' I always say. It's written in the stars,"
God said.

"You did create Jesus," I said.

"Have to admit I did. Catholics, Lutherans, Calvinists, Wesleyans,
Presbyterians, Methodists. I could go on forever. The Arabs and Muslims
don't seem to have much luck evolving either. They just always have to
have yet one more sect."

"True," I say. "Jesus, Mohammed, and Buddha flashed on what's
going on, and then people take it and boil it down to babies and battles,
no matter what the source of the religion is."

"Oh, come on," God said. "We're making headway. Only 20 percent of the people in the world are really poor today, compared to 40 percent in 1970."

"Where did you read that?" I said.

"The *New York Times*. They're always the ones researching this kind of thing."

"Well, finally that's sort of necessary, but in my own experience people seem to be most concerned with their status here on earth. Not about even how happy they are."

"Happy schmappy," God said. "It's even a bigger deal than that. But to get back to love and sex. You fall in love, you have sex, you have orgasms, you are transported to a state that you know is more important than anything else you will experience. And you will never have that if you are not brave enough to love someone who is all wrong as far as other people are concerned. And frequently they are right, you know. Everything about it except the sex is a mess," God said.

"It's true. Certainly when it comes to being fulfilled emotionally and sexually, a sense of humor is not a must," I said.

"It can even get in the way," God said. "Sex isn't funny."

I gave God an appraising look. "You're not so dumb," I said.

"I have my moments," God said. "I guess what I'm trying to say is that people have to get to a point where they will take some chances and not want to be safe all the time. It really looks like everyone would be better off if you just tell them what to do. You folks are on a test run. Let's just hope you figure some things out before you burn the planet up."

(Some of the)
Men in My Life

My Sailor Lover

My first real lover I met aboard ship in the Navy. He was an enlisted man. I was an officer, although we were close in age. The thing I remember most about him sexually was that although he had no wish to continue our homosexual affair after he left me to return to college, it was often he who wanted to explore sex activities.

When we were living in New York in a tiny apartment in Greenwich Village, he was asleep in the bed near me as I sat on the floor polishing my shoes. Was I preparing to go to church? I looked and his erect penis was poking out of the bedclothes immediately in front of my face. A fraternity brother of mine was asleep in the sitting room a few feet away, and the door was open between the rooms. I did not take him into my mouth but now, of course, I wish I had just kicked the door shut and done him the favor.

Riding in the backseat of a car driven by friends, he would take my hand and place it on his crotch, where he would become erect. He would do me the same favor.

I still speak to him very occasionally and he gets no pleasure from it. He always claimed when he was with me that sex was not a major part of his life, and yet, and yet, and yet. I have the feeling that there was a great deal there to explore that he never explored. He became a successful lawyer in the Midwest. Married and had children. But did any of those people know him the way I did? Did he forget the man he was when he was with me? I wrote a novel where he was the main character. I sent it to him but he told me he never read it. It's not good: refusing to know who you are.

Fenil

He did a threesome with a policeman and his wife several times. He stopped when the policeman wanted to meet without the wife.

I felt Fenil would hold me from sliding over into death. And when I did go, it would be just like slipping around the corner. And I would stay waiting there for him.

I must say this of Fenil: He is the only person in my life with whom I do not feel alone. I do not feel alone when I am with him.

Peter

He said: "Being involved with you is like the Agatha Christie novel *Ten Little Indians*. One by one I have to get rid of the competition."

He said: "When I fuck you, that *is* the commitment."

Traveling with Peter is like taking *Aida* on the road. He brings everything he might possibly want or need. Including sex fetish objects.

He said: "When I get excited, it gets a size bigger." My reaction: "They come in sizes? I guess they do."

Never travel with anyone if you are not sharing the same room. Peter always insists we share a double bed wherever we are. This is good and great of him.

My relationship with Peter is intimate without being romantic. He has always understood that I am not in love with him. But we have a kind of close understanding that usually only occurs later in a relationship with someone who was once a big romance. I can be crossing a hotel room and suddenly Peter will open his arms and hold me very close.

Once when he asked me, "Do you love me?" I told him, "I'm in love with your thighs." With every lover you explore new things about yourself and the way you can relate to someone else. There has been a kind of interdependency, although I know he is not really sexually excited by me at all. He likes younger men and there is something about paying for their services that he finds exciting.

His big plus is that he is very well educated, knowledgeable about the arts, and motivated to see and explore sites that interest him historically. Most of his weekends in Germany he goes by himself to some obscure town to see a church, a painting, a monastery that he has read about or seen pictures of. And this is largely self-taught. These are not things he studied in school. Traveling with him has never been any problem, as he is always interested in exploring. We went to Salzburg to see the famous Tiepolo ceiling there in the bishop's palace. An extraordinary gigantic ceiling over a vast staircase where the heavens rise and rise and rise. The largest painted ceiling the artist ever did. I don't think there is an artist today who could paint something like this in such faultless perspective. Tiepolo is my favorite painter and Peter is probably the only man I know who even knows who Tiepolo was. Peter falls somewhere between being an intimate companion and an interesting friend.

Our most recent sexual forays seem to be mostly dutiful on his part, and for myself I can't help but feel that I am in bed with the wrong person. Your body knows better than you do where it should be.

Grant Radke

Grant's mind seeks refuge in details. As with most of my nephews and nieces, you can hardly mention anything he has ever heard of.

In Venice with Grant on an outside terrace at night in the great piazza in front of San Marco, the orchestra played "Lucky to Be Loving You." The best moment.

I think the thing that bothered me most about Grant is that the men he preferred to sleep with were not even vaguely in the same ballpark as me. Uneducated, no longer young, so-so bodies. They seemed to be somewhere for Grant to stick his dick. Not anyone with whom he would really have some kind of relationship.

And yet every time our relationship shifted toward becoming sexual it would shift away, as I would not do my part, which I recognized. There was something there that I knew I wouldn't like.

A number of times I flew out to Kansas, where he was rescuing a company from self-destruction. He came to my motel with a bottle of wine to watch a movie, and somehow I just didn't feel like crawling all over him. There and also in Miami Beach he got really drunk at dinner several times and I had to make sure he got home safely. Was that a kind of invitation for me to come home with him and see what was cooking? I didn't think so at the time.

It's a curious thing, isn't it? This reluctance many men have to mix intimacy and sex. Perhaps it's some feeling that sex is degrading and you can't have respect and admiration for someone with whom you have sex.

It is strange. I know Grant very well and I really like to be with him. His wish to have power and control over his life and his enterprising spirit are all attractive elements in his personality. He has thrown himself into establishing an international empire, opening offices in China and France and England. It's that chance-taking energy I like. You don't find it in many people. I told him recently on the phone he was the only man I would have married, even without knowing him better sexually. But that is of course no longer the case.

Frederick

His only joke I remember: I said, "Jesus never told jokes." Frederick replied, "Maybe he was German."

There's so much to say about Frederick that I haven't said. He was of Norwegian stock. He had a bulky, overweight mother and an unassertive father. I think they met when she was a cook in a lumber camp. He had an attractive younger brother who disappeared mysteriously along the Pacific Coast, his abandoned car parked beside a deserted beach.

I remember inviting Frederick and his mother to lunch when she was visiting in New York and seeing them entering the restaurant. She in a suit and hat I think she wore rarely. He is standing beside her, suddenly the ill-at-ease boy from North Dakota, which was what he really was underneath all the sexual glamour.

After his mother's death Frederick's father came to live in New York. He stayed in some kind of workmen's residence, got a job as a carpenter or a plumber right away, earned a living, paid his bills, and saw his sons perhaps weekly. I am always confounded by the usual family relationship, where they see each other, want to stay in touch with each other, but never discuss what their relationship really is. Or even seem aware of it. Never express affection, never advance in the way that even the most usual friendship does. To love someone and not grow closer to them, I cannot understand it. It seems to me so many lives remain unlived. I cannot stand it really.

Frederick never had a career or a job focus. He drifted from one kind of part-time work to another. I think his focus was really on his sex life. He had a beautiful body and a very beautiful penis. He enjoyed sex greatly but I don't think he ever felt much of what could be called romantic love. He had a brief affair with a young Frenchman once and said to me, "I think with Pierre I'm feeling what you talk about when you talk about love." But that was the only time I ever heard him refer to love.

He became someone who welcomed many sexual partners and also said to me later in his life, "I must have had a yard of cock in me in the last two weeks." Even so, our sex life continued on somewhere separate from all that activity. I think the fact that he relished sexual intercourse so much made me feel the same way. His fulfillment was my fulfillment. I think I am still very much that way with Fenil, who otherwise is nothing at all like Frederick.

Two Men I Loved I Forgot to Tell You About

While I was in my late fifties and early sixties I was emotionally involved with two men, but we never became lovers. One was a young man named Gil, Gilbert. A much younger Midwesterner wandering astray in Europe. He came to Paris with a friend of mine who was working in Germany. I understood that they were lovers. When I saw him coming through customs with his shouldery, hunky walk I knew he spelled trouble and avoided getting to know him well.

But when Gil came back to Paris, I helped him get a job where I worked, and he lived with me. I fell very much in love with him, which I had absolutely no intention of doing. I was in my fifties, and he was in his early twenties. It was embarrassing. When I fall in love with someone it always lasts at least ten years.

It was really awful. He left Paris and went to an island in the Mediterranean to work in a hotel. I called every hotel on the island until I found him. And it wasn't a small island. One of my friends near my age said, "I'm really jealous." It was that sort of thing: you see a friend embroiled in a hopeless romance and you just want to shake them and say, "Wake up." I began to come out of it when a couple I knew came to a Sunday brunch and she said, seeing his photo framed on a bureau in my bedroom, "You should at least put his picture away." As I began to come out of it, I wrote a book about the experience. I still remember it as being awful. Fenil could have gone this way except that Fenil just took over like a man and made it real.

The other man was a neighbor in Miami Beach. I was conducting a signature collection in a battle to get a noise ordinance established in this town. Night clubs had suddenly shot up along the beach, one right below my windows. Without an ordinance they blasted music until the early dawn and made the nights hideous not only for me but for many retirees living in the large nearby buildings. Scavenging for names, I knocked at a door and a half-dressed man answered. Imagine a big Mel Gibson. A very handsome guy, Bob. As simple as that. Single. Working at some dumb computer job. I ran into him in a nearby coffee shop later and made an effort to chat with him. I think he was lonely. I can pull men into my orbit when I make an effort. I needed a model for a little publicity job. I told him he should model and used him. Actually he photographed very well. I took him to New York for test shots. I took him to Paris to talk to agencies there to see if a modeling career was possible. The agencies were interested, but Bob did not have the drive for it. I was the one with the drive for it, but I never communicated that to him.

Certainly Bob knew I was interested in him, and I think that interest did move him away from the computer into working on the boats that prowl back and forth from Miami to the Bahamas with passengers on fishing trips. He really liked that and got a captain's license. He sent me photographs displaying his great body and a giant fish. Bob was a honey. He still is. But I always kept one foot on the ground and did not repeat my useless little romance with Gil.

Strange, isn't it? These frustrating and pointless little loves that one could clearly expect for a gay man moving from his fifth decade to his sixth. And then, the totally unexpected emotional life of my seventies.

Mark

Mark was the lover who fulfilled me. We were lovers for ten years, and in that period I met up with my sexual destiny. He was the lover with whom I had simultaneous orgasms. I never hear anyone discuss orgasms, but there is something about the two of you falling through space together locked in one another's arms that makes other kinds of sexual contact seem infinitely lesser.

For the years I knew him Mark was young and beautiful. They were the years his theater career was advancing. He could sing and dance and looked a lot like Tyrone Power. Not very tall, but that was not a big drawback in the New York theater world of that time. He was Italian, and there has to be a link to the Latin American world I know in South America. Of course a lot of those men are of Italian and Portuguese descent also. Mark liked to get out of all his clothes and wander around. All kinds of sexual positions were interesting to him, and he actually remained focused on his sex partner during sex, instead of drifting off into that bang-bang-bang thing most men do.

I'm not experienced enough to really draw any major conclusions, but it seems to me men of Northern European backgrounds are always slightly embarrassed about sex. The closer to the equator the less so. Is that Puritanism vs. Catholicism? Puritans can't be forgiven their sins.

Toward the end of his life Mark was a self-proclaimed semi-invalid, but I was with him in a car once and he turned from the wheel and said, "You know, I really loved you." And for a moment that melding together was there and I remembered how much I had loved him, too.

I have one test for deciding whether I want to know someone or not, let alone fall in love with them. Do they use the packing light for anything but packing? The packing light is the central overhead light in a room, usually a bedroom, often a hotel bedroom. In its light everything looks bleak and desperate and temporary. Put on the low bedside lights, turn off the packing light, and voilà! Suddenly everything is warm and cozy and looks like home.

But for many people there is no difference. They can lie down and read the paper under the packing light and apparently feel perfectly at ease. *That spells insensitivity.* They will never notice when you're depressed or not enjoying sex. It is a very sad discovery, particularly among younger relatives. You know they're doomed to go through life viewing it dimly, coldly. Can someone become aware of the difference? In my experience, only when they are with me, not by themselves. And then they may only be humoring me.

Voyeurama

Has anyone ever done a book on masturbation fantasies? I'd love to read it. It's something gay men rarely talk about. I guess the implicit understanding is that each of us is getting so much sex we don't really have the time or need to masturbate.

But, of course, everyone does. A whole lot. Precipitated by the AIDS crisis. At least you're not going to contract some fatal disease from your own hand.

In my own case, my fantasies have always involved real people. I've never been able to get excited by imagining sex with Superman or Batman or even film stars. Well, maybe the young Mel Gibson. Mel has, or at least had, a great ass. Which he showed off in one of those *policier* movies of his. The one with Patsy Kensit, the English attempt at an actress. She had one great scene where he finds her dead, tied to a post underwater. She looked great. I always wondered how they did that. Air tube? What?

I have never found porn stars worthy of masturbation fantasies either. Supposedly men respond to visual sexual stimulation, women to physical. Perhaps I'm such a woman that looking at someone on film does not excite me unduly. Having him plopped down on top of me is what is really thrilling. Certainly a great kisser will get the best results with me.

For those reasons, I am guessing my fantasies have, for the most part, recapitulated sex I have actually had: my high school lover, my lover in the navy, my lover of thirty years who was a dancer, the great love of my life (the hot Italian actor), a guy I slept with regularly who was very handsome, had a great body, but never did excite me all that much. I had been spoiled. I think the excitement of having sex with someone with whom you are in love spoils you for more routine encounters. Love is the greatest of all aphrodisiacs. It spoils you so that plain garden-variety lust seems like a second-rate experience. Now as I am older, I hesitate to sleep with younger men because it looks bad. Your bodies are too dissimilar. There is always the possibility they are just being kind or perhaps hoping it will result in greater financial stability. And since seeing my friends develop crushes on twenty-year-old waiters and only slightly older gym trainers and being embarrassed for them, I would be embarrassed for myself if I did the same thing.

Actually, I don't think my friends are so sexually attracted to these younger men; they just want to be seen as still in the running. And what I also suspect is, you are attracted to the age group where your own meaningful sex life left off. If your last real sex was in your early twenties, that's the age group you'll be attracted to.

Even worse are those guys who like young teenagers and children. They discovered sex then and never got past it. No hot adult romances for them.

Now in my masturbation fantasy, my lover does not look uneasy. He actually has the slightly rapacious expression he got when sex was imminent. He was a great lover of sex. He's dead now. So is the man who is seated on the nearby couch, my friend Harding. Now in my new scenario, I rise and seat myself beside Harding on the couch and say to him, "Come over here. I've always wanted to sit between two men and have both hands on their hard-ons." My lover comes over, I open both their flies, pull out penises that are already beginning to enlarge, and start masturbating them slightly. It is something like skiing.

They both begin to move their pelvises rhythmically, throwing their arms over my shoulders. Three buddies. I suggest to my lover, "Move to the other side of Harding and let's start taking his clothes off." My lover does, and as he does, I start removing his clothes. Harding takes over his own slow masturbation.

I take off both men's shoes and socks in order to remove their pants. I somehow find that one of the sexiest parts of having sex. Their bare feet emerging, although I am definitely not a shrimp queen. No toe

sucking for me. Or having it done. That's more like some sort of
cleansing ritual than a sexual one for me.

The other very sexy moment is when your sex partner lifts his hips so
you can pull off his underpants. It's a sort of gesture that always tells me
he really wants sex. He's not just being cooperative, nice, or whatever.

Harding makes the hip-lifting movement for my lover. I just pull
my standing lover's briefs down to his ankles, and he steps out of them.
I put him in my mouth for a moment. He says, "Would you mind
closing the inside shutters so we're sure no one can see in." I cross the
room and do so. I know the handsome man, Harding, is a great aficio-
nado of being fucked, and my lover kneels in front of the couch, places
Harding's ankles on his shoulders and moves in to insert his very sizeable
penis in Harding. He doesn't put on a condom because this is a fantasy.
And it was before the AIDS crisis when they looked as they do in my
fantasy. This is one of those fantasies where both parties actually knew
each other. It doesn't pull together widely disparate time periods.

In the fantasy, my lover plunges more deeply and more rapidly into
the man on the couch, bracing himself with one arm on each side of his
body. The couch isn't fictional. It's a couch on which I've had a fair
amount of sex. I have taken my clothes off and am seated on the couch
masturbating Harding as he is being fucked. I don't worry about
stains. (A) This is a fantasy, and (B) even if it wasn't, Harding's buttocks
are far enough off the couch they're not touching the very expensive
upholstery.

My lover comes very deeply inside his partner, tipped back into the
couch. This isn't a porn movie. I always found the money shot much
less interesting than watching someone have an orgasm. Men who have
no problem performing sex while others watch have schooled themselves to mask the moment of total vulnerability. But an orgasm is a
powerful thing. It's impossible to be stone-faced through it, and in that
moment, you can actually see who this man is, all defenses down.

With some men, it is the only moment when you truly can be one
with who they are. And perhaps I am exercising my female side. The
dominating male collapses, and for those few moments, I am the
stronger one. I have brought him to this. Of course, the ideal scene is

when you both have orgasms at the same time and you go sailing off into the stars together.

I use this fantasy frequently. It seems not to run dry of inspiration. Sometimes we go upstairs to my bedroom. Sometimes there is frontal entry there, Harding's butt propped up with large bed pillows. In actuality, he liked that.

Sometimes Harding is kneeling on all fours for rear entry. Sometimes my lover is kneeling for rear entry, and Harding enters him, and I enter Harding from the rear, all at the same time.

Sometimes in the frontal entry position, I kneel over Harding and place my penis in his mouth and take his in mine. This is a true fantasy as Harding did not like to give oral sex although he liked receiving it very much.

And sometimes when my lover is the recipient of frontal entry, lying on his back on the pillow, I do the same thing. He, too, liked receiving oral sex but also liked proffering it. He really was an expert and beautiful sensualist, and I was very lucky to have slept with him for thirty years until his death. On his deathbed when he lay there very ill, I looked at his unusually blackened and diminished penis and thought how much pleasure it had given him and many others in his lifetime. He never achieved fulfillment in the public world, but far more than most in the private one. Do you think there is a connection there? When men are rebuffed by, or don't have the necessary skills to manipulate the exterior world, do they then become more skilled with arts of sensuality and sexuality? I think so. It is their arena of success.

As time goes by, I find I am adding new characters to the masturbation fantasies. All of which essentially take place in a house I once owned in New York City.

There was a fraternity brother from college with whom I shared a bed, and I once woke up to find him sprawled across me, ostensibly asleep. Let's call him Bill.

Now I resurrected his visit and imagined him visiting me at my own house and sometimes the scenario involved only him and me. He atop me, eyes closed, surging inside of me.

Sometimes after several visits, the fantasies included introducing him to my lover and to Harding. Sometimes there were foursomes, with my lover atop Harding, Bill atop me. Bill loved all these shenanigans.

I also resurrected my lover from the days when I was a young naval officer. I imagined he, too, was in New York on business. Came to call with his curls, blue eyes, and buff, bulgy, big white body still intact also.

He, too, enjoyed climbing aboard my slim, ex-dancer lover and experimented with sitting on his large penis as he lay beneath him. I put his penis in my mouth, while he straddled my lover and moved vigorously up and down, and I placed my own penis in my lover's mouth. Fantasy or not, it was exactly the kind of thing my lover would have enjoyed doing, although we were never involved in a threesome.

My naval lover left me before our own experimentation went very far, and he always claimed I had led him into homosexual acts he really didn't want to perform. He married and begot children shortly after we separated. However, every instance of his fondling my crotch in the backseat of a car driven by naval friends, or kissing me in the kitchen at someone else's party, or wanting a blowjob while a college friend was in the living room a few feet away were all instigated by him. Perhaps my masturbation fantasies were not far afield from what might have been his own.

Lastly, back into my fantasy life came the boy I had conducted an active sex life with in my hometown until the age of eighteen. Ricky had a kind of Greek, godlike body, with skin so pale and thin, so little body fat. One could see the blue veins coursing in his arms and thighs and partially in his lower abdomen when he was playing basketball shirtless.

Now I think of him. He was an eager and heartless bed partner, and I could easily imagine him visiting New York as a midlife adult. A man in his forties still possessed of a fine physique and a head of hair.

In what now seems a pattern, he first was atop me, then graduated to sharing a bed with my lover and me. He was an experienced lover in high school and had no problems in my fantasies with administering and receiving oral sex, with entry and being entered. The entire repertoire seems to suit him, as a gymnast wants to display his skills or a tightrope walker is pleased to show off his skills. He was a show-off. He would have made a great gay man.

Recently, I had the fantasy that his father had appeared with him, as had an older brother, who had frolicked with me several times in our school years.

I was pleased as an adult to be able to offer myself as an adult to his father, which I did. And in a prolonged fantasy, the four of us cavorted, with father and sons exchanging oral sex, my friend having frontal entry with his father, who welcomed it, and finally my friend having sex with me as his brother did with his father, we two couples side by side on my bed.

My fantasies have become more exotic if not in the superpervert category. But never have I introduced an imaginary playmate from a porn video or magazine, or someone I admired that I never actually slept with.

The Question

I had a teacher in college who said of Hemingway short stories, "They are just an arc. But if you know the arc you know the entire circle." I wonder. Here's a fragment of a short story I wrote that seems important in the exploration of these later years. Perhaps this is an arc of an arc . . .

*A*re *you gay?"*

Crandall Rand raised his hand. I nodded to him. "Are you gay, Mr. Waffington?" he said. The class froze. I sat down on the corner of my desk.

"That is an interesting question, Crandall," I said. "Does it have some kind of distant relationship to American Poets II, which is the subject we are discussing today?"

"Not really," Crandall said.

I felt sorry for him. He was one of those thickly built college students who looks like he should be a football player but isn't. And will certainly be doomed to a lifetime of getting heavier and heavier, physically as well as in spirit.

Crandall went on. "But if you were, wouldn't that affect the way you perceive the poets we're studying?"

"It might very well," I said. "But I'm trying to get the interpretations from you." I gestured toward the class. "And from them." Men like Crandall Rand reminded me of snapping turtles. Their ugly little eyes have a touch of intelligence. They venture forth a bit from their shell but are always ready to recoil back.

"But even more important, I think we should discuss today not why you asked the question, but whether questions like that are appropriate in a college class. It might have a lot to do with sexuality, but is it really studying the work of different men and women who wrote about many different things in a different time and place?" The class was still frozen. Being gay wasn't a subject this bunch was ready to be relaxed about. We were deep in the Corn Belt.

I shut my book. "Our class is about poetry, so let me propose some questions and you will tell me if they are appropriate here. And if not, why not. And if so, why so."

I know my classes here at Buttress College are popular because I'm from out of state. I've lived in New York. I came here from Miami. I have a house in South America. This all makes me quite an exotic bird, and my vocabulary keeps my classes from being boring. The other teachers hate me, partly because I couldn't care less if my classes are popular or not and they are desperate to fill their classes. Why is it that people of this type like dressing in brown and decorating their homes in brown? No one looks good in brown. Let me correct that. No one in brown wouldn't look better in a different color.

"So, let's see. What if I were to ask Betty here," I indicated Betty Windsham in the front row, "if her breasts were the same size." There was an indrawn gasp in the room.

"Now mind you, I'm not asking Betty. I'm just saying, 'What if.' So you can't all go running out of here saying I asked Betty Windsham if her breasts were the same size. I am not asking her, so I don't want campus gossip playing back later that I did."

The class looked discomfited. I had pulled the rug out from under them. Class had been exciting. Suddenly class wasn't exciting. Betty in the front row did not seem to be discomfited. She was sitting up straight and under her mud-colored button-front sweater I could see she had a swell pair of knockers. What is that they say about college girls? "They're just as big as real women except dumber." In Betty's case it couldn't have been truer.

"And how about you, Crandall? We could ask about your penis size.

I could ask you how you feel you compare to the other guys in the class. Mind you, I am not asking. Is that clear to everyone? I could ask, but I'm not. And we could go around the class and ask each and every person something that would be very important to them. 'Do you feel you have enough pubic hair?' 'Or not enough?' 'Is there a part of your body you don't want anyone to see?' 'Are you worried about premature balding?' 'Do you think your mother loves you?' 'And you her?' And the same questions relating to your father. How about, 'Are you a virgin?' 'Kind of want to be?' 'Kind of don't want to be?' Girls, would you consider getting a man to marry you by getting pregnant by him? These are all highly charged questions that perhaps no one has ever asked you. And yes, of course, there is 'Are you gay?'"

I had the little dopes squirming in their seats. This is what they obviously thought about all the time, to hell with Emily Dickinson and her sitting around upstairs.

Maureen Moorestick stood up, tucking her book under her arm. "I think this class should be over. It's gotten far too personal."

"Sit down, Maureen," I said with authority. "What does the rest of the class think? Let's take a quick vote. Who else wants to call it a day?" Several girls raised their hands, but the boys, particularly the trouble-makers, kept their hands to themselves. This was going to be a memorable day, and they wanted to see where it was going.

I felt like a bit of a shit by not promptly saying, "Yes, I'm gay, what of it?" but that would have put us on a confrontational basis. I wanted the class to end with everyone feeling very adult and scorning Crandall Rand a bit.

Montevideo

When I mention that I live in Montevideo part of the year there is always much confusion. Do I mean Montenegro, near Croatia? Do I mean Monterrey in Mexico on the gulf? No, I mean the capitol of Uruguay. Which just causes more confusion, as everyone knows that Uruguay and Paraguay exist but are not at all sure where they are. If they know a little something, they usually think that it is Paraguay that is the little pie-shaped country caught between Argentina and Brazil. I can't say I was any better before I went there.

I always tell people that it was a poem by Jorge Luis Borges that led me to Montevideo. I did read the famous Argentinean poet, and I did read a poem that said something like "There is magic in the streets of Montevideo," but I think it was more than that. I had worked in Buenos Aires doing television commercials and knew that Montevideo was across the river. Something in my past has always made it seem very romantic, and I think Borges just confirmed it for me.

So at Christmas as I was approaching seventy, I grabbed a friend, and we went to Montevideo. I had read an article in *Wallpaper* magazine on Montevideo, and we stayed at the hotel they recommended. A small place in the old city where each room was decorated on a different theme, all of them awkward. Mine was nautical and Herb's military, as I remember.

It was a chilly December although technically already summer there. As we left the hotel in the evening, the pedestrian street Sarandi was empty and cold under its streetlights. We pulled our jackets about us as we went out to find a restaurant.

Suddenly there was a group of dancers in the empty street. They were leaping and rolling to the snap-snap-snap of their choreographer's fingers. The wind blew from the river. It was cold and empty and lonely yet there they were, doing their Martha Graham contractions and bent knee leaps. I said to my friend, "Is this an art attack?" It was completely magical and made me love Montevideo from the start. That was the first big mystery of Montevideo, which was solved the following day when I saw the festival that filled that long walkway on the day before Christmas. There were singers and bands and jugglers and artists and there among them, the modern dance troupe, now in costume and with music. It didn't spoil the mystery for me, and there were more, many more. Soon I was to see a large and empty house, buy it, and start my new life there.

The men of Montevideo are, for the most part, lean and hang onto their bodies. Blue-collar workingmen really work physically, and their bodies show it.

In the summer, the boys and young men frequently ride around on their bikes with their shirts off, and the long-torsoed Uruguayan body looks good on a bicycle. Broad shoulders tapering down to a narrow waist riding away from you down an empty street with dense trees arching overhead. Pretty beautiful. This isn't really a mystery—except why aren't more cities like this?

Men in Buenos Aires

I just came back from Buenos Aires. There are lots of sexy men there, and sexy in a different way from the men in Montevideo, who are certainly very sexy, too. Here in Montevideo, men are sexy in a kind of animalistic, unaware way. The shirts-off guys who drive the wagons collecting junk, the *botelleros*, don't seem to know how sexy they are. They are just ready to fuck because they are who they are. Buenos Aires men are different in that they seem to know quite well that they are sexy and recognize the effect they have upon you.

In Buenos Aires with friends, we had a cabdriver who brought us back from the San Telmo antique district, laughed at my Spanish, and obviously enjoyed our banter. He was young and boyish with a fringe of bangs, light brown hair, brown eyes, and pale skin. Not very Latin. Latin in the way his probably 100 percent Italian heritage created.

The men here are not like the Italians, and they are not like the Spanish. They have something else going here. The tango says so much about this culture. One of their writers wrote, "The tango is a sad idea that became a dance." I think the men suggest an understanding of attraction that is not about founding a dynasty but having an experience. North Americans ruin everything with their idea that each love affair is destined to last a lifetime.

At any rate, this young man wanted me to guess his age. I guessed twenty-five. He looked twenty-eight. It's always best to go younger. Even a lot. He was thirty-one. I marveled. I asked where he thought the world was going. He told me that he vacationed all over the Caribbean, which I thought was unusual. Perhaps someone takes him there. He works twelve hours a day, from six in the morning until six at night, and then goes swimming. He said that he was like a sailor; he had loves in many ports and did not wish to have a wife. He worked six days a week. If I had had any reason to be in Buenos Aires, I would have taken his name and number. He would have been worth adding to the men I've known in my life.

When I told my friend Richard about the cabdriver, he said, "You are an outrageous flirt." And I said, "I don't think being interested in someone else comes under the heading of flirtation. At worst, I would have been interested in falling in love with him. Not him falling in love with me. Flirtation is when you are trying to draw someone else's interest to you." Richard did not understand that. Certainly I understand that no one gets enough real attention, even attractive men. And there's nothing wrong with leaving a man with the impression that you found him interesting, even fascinating, and that somewhere down the line you might sleep with him. That doesn't require a lot from you.

I've recently met the British ambassador to Uruguay and his wife, a woman who certainly knows how to direct her attention fully at a person. She has been studying tango but doesn't like the fact that her partner must hold her close and he can be anyone. I told her, "If having a stranger hold you close is bothering you, you have to get over that." I've been mauled about by men all my life, and I don't feel any the less fresh for it. They're doing the mauling.

Another beautiful man I saw in Buenos Aires only had one leg. A beautiful boy actually. I was waiting to cross the gigantic Avenida Julio 9, which I think is perhaps the widest avenue in the world. Perhaps there is something in Beijing wider. At the light, there was a young man in a wheelchair, seeming very undecided about crossing by himself. I asked him if I could help him and pushed him across. The other people around us, including my friends, hadn't really noticed him. Strange, isn't it? Most people never seem to notice anyone in a wheelchair, or begging, or with some physical defect.

It took two lights to cross, and on the other side I asked him in which direction he was going. And if he would like some money. He said he would, and I gave him some. When he looked up at me, he was of a really extravagant dark handsomeness. Maybe seventeen or eighteen. And I thought again, if I were in Buenos Aires he would be someone I would try to add to my life and try to add myself to his. How is it more people don't do this? And, of course, I feel guilty because it is my reaction to beauty. I feel like being supportive to all lost people but am moved to action when they are beautiful. It's cheap on my part, but that is the way I am. And as most people are, I am sure.

The last man I noticed in Buenos Aires was the man who changed money at the Buquebus terminal, where I was taking the boat back to Montevideo. After the chaotic activities of checking in and then having someone stamp the papers for all my purchases in Buenos Aires, and then going to the cash windows to get my refunds and then going to the exchange to get the Argentinean pesos changed into dollars or Montevidean pesos, I was a bit winded from all the hurly-burly.

The man behind the exchange window was very darkly handsome in the true Latin way. He, too, thought my Spanish amusing and smiled with a really wonderful smile. He was wearing a wedding ring, but there was something there of wanting to be known better. Again, if I were to be in Buenos Aires, I would have told him he should be photographed and to contact me and would have left him my card. He was out of the ordinary but will be there in the exchange booth without notice forever. Unless someone like myself drags him out of there.

These cities are not like their counterparts in the Northern Hemisphere. If you take someone out of his world into another one north of the equator, he can be very knowing and realize he is playing a very specific hand to better his lot in the world. These men don't know this here because opportunity is so limited. I think that it is the lack of opportunity that bothers me here and makes me want to change the lot of these people economically. And thereby changing all I like about this part of the world.

And yet again, my young cabdriver told me, "You have to understand apropos of where the world is going, that if we have enough to eat and a roof over our heads that is sufficient to allow us to enjoy our lives." This is so different from North Americans. It is something to think about.

Before we left Buenos Aires, I spent an evening with a high-flying friend from Paris. She has worked her way through a number of big spenders and famous men. I always loved her because after she broke up with the actor Keir Dullea, who was then at the peak of his fame after starring in that early *Space Odyssey* movie, I enquired about him and she replied, "Keir Dullea, gone tomorrow."

I left Peter, who had been with me, in the hotel room, and when I returned from my friend's, I found him still there. But after we got into bed and turned out the lights he told me he had called and seen a male escort. He likes to pay, and it may involve using props and costumes. I don't think it went very well, but I dismissed it.

I think he has a mindset that he shouldn't just enjoy sex for itself; it should be serving some purpose. When we have sex, I think he concentrates on "underdoing" it to keep his attention on his partner and has a really big orgasm. He certainly divides affection and sex as two completely different activities. But a lot of gay men do that. They have men they love and men they have sex with and never the twain shall meet. I wonder if that is because they dislike being homosexual and think it's bad. Or their early religious training made them think of anything sexual as bad.

We have intimacy but it isn't at all the feelings I have for Fenil. But it is strong and not to be shunted aside as unimportant. And for me, perhaps our relationship is love but not just the romantic kind that I have been used to in the past.

A Trip

Peter and I were planning a trip together. In the summer. He wanted to revisit places in Germany he had visited in the past. He loves the mountains. I had read in the *New York Times* that nobody was going to the Dalmatian Coast because of the economic recession and the hotels were standing empty. It was supposed to be chic, and I had never been there, although my friend Catherine had been there by yacht the previous summer and only shook her head when asked about it.

Peter did not want to repeat the kind of trip we had taken the year before. A tour down the Romantic Road in Germany. I had organized it to go by train between each of the old cities, had reserved the hotels, and planned what we would do each day. It was primarily visits to the palaces of Mad King Ludwig, something I had always wanted to do. Peter found it over-organized. He prefers just setting out, staying as long as one feels like, making hotel reservations as one goes. I decided to humor him on the trip.

So first we met in Munich. My favorite thing was seeing the Amalienburg at the summer palace. This small lodge in the forest contains what I think is the most beautiful room in Europe. I particularly like Rococo style, and the main room is a fantasy in silver and pale blue with huge, glittering chandeliers dipping down from the ceiling. Rococo and its fragile filigree is usually in gold. This room is in silver and not sumptuous but more like seeing light across the waves. Hard to pin down what the surface actually was.

From Munich we went to see Peter's aunt and uncle in Vienna. I had been there frequently in my advertising days. Now it seems more internationalized with the shops one sees everywhere. I always said if worst came to worst, I would go to Vienna and open a loden coat store. One that also sold those green-brimmed hats with a feather tucked into the band. Everyone in Vienna wore loden coats then. The streets were filled with that green felty fabric. Now I am not so sure. Vienna may have moved past the loden coat.

And on we went. To a mountain village perched on a very black, flat, glassy lake. The mountain that rose behind the village had been home to an early lead mine, active in the Roman days. There was something brooding about this place, and the lake looked like an excellent place in which to dispose of a body. We went from there to another mountain resort by train, traveling through the very countryside where I had shot the Jontue television commercial maybe twenty or thirty years ago. Lisa Palmer, running endlessly in her flimsy chiffon dress, listening to a hunting horn and finally finding that handsome man on horseback. A gay man's dream. Sunny fields, mountainsides jammed with flowers. I felt a little nostalgic. Not much.

Peter does love the mountains. I myself don't like to be that far away from bookstores and newspapers. He had filmed here and remembered the dramatic forest clearings, steep cliffs, pine-lined roads. Perhaps I have just seen a lot more of nature than he has. My nephew was going camping once, and I said to his mother, my sister, "Did you ever like to go camping?" She answered, "If you weren't brought up in the country as we were, you'd like that sort of thing." Exactly.

In Dubrovnik, I keeled over in front of a church from dehydration and much worried Peter. He dragged me back to the hotel and called a doctor. I heard him explain to the doctor that his "elderly" friend had fainted from the heat. When words like these are dropped, you understand what is really going on with you and your "boyfriend." I don't think either of these words is actually very definitive.

Leaving Dubrovnik was a nightmare joke. We were booked on a night boat crossing the Adriatic to Bari. At a café in the morning I casually glanced at the tickets and discovered the ship was leaving at 4:30 in the afternoon and arriving at 10:30 in the evening, instead of departing at ten at night. Scurrying took place. Cancel the plan to spend the day touring islands by boat. Rush to a café to go online and find a hotel in Bari. Get our asses to the boat dock. This was entirely the capricious Croatian mode of living, as the boat had been reserved for months. The schedule had been changed with no word to anyone. It only went twice a week so being aboard was imperative. To Peter's credit, in a pinch, he remains calm and does his duty.

We arrived at Bari and found the boat docking far from the center of the city and two taxis waiting for the several hundred voyagers. I said to Peter, "You run and get one of those taxis. I will follow with the bags." I got to the taxi and found a group of travelers arguing with the driver about the fare. We climbed in and left for our hotel.

The next day, we arrived at the train terminal to find the train was completely booked and nothing was available until late in the afternoon for Naples. Peter's idea of traveling without plans was beginning to wear very thin for me.

I liked Naples and loved Capri. I want to go back. The water was cleaner than any I've ever seen. The seaside resort further up the coast, where Peter had summered as a child, was all right. Wealthy Italians, very heterosexual or faux heterosexual, much like their class equivalent in France. A sandy beach, but again, "Why am I here when I live in Miami Beach?"

The final straw that broke my back was our train from Milan to Paris. Peter hates flying, so we trained everywhere. Arriving on Friday, we found that the French train office where we had to pick up the tickets was actually blocks from the train station. It closed at five o'clock for the weekend.

When we arrived, the scene was much like the deck of the *Titanic* as it slowly sank. Everyone who had to pick up a ticket for the entire weekend was standing in endless lines for the lackadaisical clerks. When we got to the clerk, we found that because the reservation had been made by a friend in France they could not honor it, as my American Express card was different from his. Thank God for cell phones. I called him, and miraculously, he was still in his office in Paris and spoke to the clerk and gave her his American Express card number. Why am I telling you all this? What phase of the moon could we possibly have been in?

And then, we arrived in our first-class car to find that actually it was second class and another couple was already ensconced in it. I have to say, Peter takes all these travel debacles very calmly. I think it reveals a deep rift in our personalities. I am American. I expect things to go right and be well executed. Peter, although American, has lived in Europe such a large part of his life that he accepts as normal the disorganized, illogical, thoughtless manner in which things are done.

The customer is not always right in Europe. You may pay, but it is entirely at the convenience of the seller. Somehow I expect this in South America. I think Europe has been given a chance to get up to speed and seems to be blowing it. Or am I wrong? Is what you eat and long vacations more important?

People who live in former monarchies have little plan to change their class. They are there, plan to stay there, and have little expectation of moving upward to another class and having more money. In the United States, we do because we are not uncomfortable in a higher class. Finally, we are all the same people, just some with more cash. And the next generation may quickly sink back to the level their ancestors came from. With Peter, I see these differences in thinking.

Peter and I parted in Paris, curiously no closer or more distant than when we began this trip. It was my idea. I will not have this kind of idea again.

When I Was Very Small

When I was very small I would sleep in the same bed with my grandmother in Holland, Michigan, and I would hear the night train blowing its whistle and feel very, very sad.

Another Trip

At Christmastime, I planned to go to Salvador, Bahia, with Fenil and his son. I had organized this several months in advance and found when I called the travel agent that his wife and he were actually far up the Amazon and his office was closed. I couldn't even get a visa for Brazil, as I didn't have any flight information or hotel reservations. The blight of my trip with Peter seemed to be already spreading to this trip.

Finally, my messages left at the travel bureau (I know, I know, you are saying, why in heaven do I still have a travel agent and am not doing this all online?) got me a return call from a pleasant but unknowledgeable intern. She completely misunderstood the project, and because her boss had forgotten to get flights for Fenil and his son, the ticket prices had since doubled, and when we arrived in Salvador, the hotel was located on a cliff over the loudest nightclubs in town. I was beginning to think that God was trying to tell me something. I should not be traveling.

Salvador is the old original capitol of Brazil. All of its publicity suggests that it is a quaint old place high on cliffs over the sea. Winding cobblestone streets pass through pastel-colored colonial buildings. This exists but is somewhat lost amid the three million inhabitants crammed into red block shantytowns with tin roofs that crawl over the hills and gullies that lie behind and around the ancient town.

Salvador is a wild town filled with wild drivers. Because it was the landing place of all the many slaves imported into Brazil, the population is certainly at least 50 percent black. Salvador teems with activity, and that I like. Its history I found fascinating, but museum after museum was closed for the holidays. Good restaurants were rare, the hotel was unsleepable, and Fenil and his boy were not having a good time. So we departed to a seaside resort, still within the city limits but far from the noise and wildness.

Fenil and his little boy liked this resort. They loved the large, spreading swimming pools, the organized games for children, the enormous amounts of food available at the dining room buffets. Fenil was remote and spent much of his time playing volleyball on the beach or in the pool with his child. I didn't mind, although this holiday was far from what I had had in mind.

Salvador is the only city I really wanted to see. Physically, it was pretty much what I had imagined, but it was obviously no place I could ever live, and I was disappointed in this. I was also being left alone much of the time to sit beneath an umbrella and read beside the pool. In the evening, Fenil was playing electronic and other games with younger friends he had met at the hotel.

Christmas Eve, the children received presents their parents had provided from a Santa in the hotel lobby. Santa was a large black lady, which baffled me for a moment, but then I realized that she held the littlest children on her lap and the Brazilians did not want a male Santa holding their little girls. Their machismo culture doesn't allow that.

New Year's, we were in Buenos Aires, and after two or three rather empty days of shopping and eating, Fenil told me he had a girlfriend. They had met at the beach during the winter some nine months before. She was lovely, an art teacher, his son loved her very much, etc., etc., etc. The emotional distance and boredom all fell into place.

"Let's go back to Montevideo right away," I said. And the next day, the boat spirited us back across the Platte River. Now I understood why Fenil had appropriated my bedroom in Montevideo when I wasn't there. It had more closet space.

I met Liliana. She was beautiful and kind and caring and intelligent and slender. Fenil is very lucky to have her. Her understanding is that he manages property for me, hence the large house, car, college tuition.

I let them use my beach cottage for the month of January. I had no wish to be there with them. I rented a cottage two doors away for myself and friends from Miami and Paris. I only saw them on the beach at a distance. We dined together en masse several times.

I think Fenil thought I would be the kind old uncle to this newly organized household. Or not so newly organized household. I have no intention of that. In your late seventies, everyone is trying to organize your life so that you have some kind of caregiver present. I have no intention of descending down through the years, ever more childlike. That will not be my destiny. I have a horror of that.

So what's next? There is no place for me in his life as it is presently organized, and I wish very much to have Liliana continue as a part of it. Fenil was bitterly disappointed at not being able to get a visa for the United States. Now he is heading for a solid middle-class life in Uruguay. Who am I to say that what I want is what I should get? Now I must simply wait, but there is something very much like a broken heart that I feel as I get up each morning before meditation dispels it and I go on with my day.

On Bariloche, Argentina

I went to Bariloche, high in the Andes in Argentina, to go fishing with Fenil and his brother. We rendezvoused in Buenos Aires, and then flew to Bariloche, which is a two-hour flight. It is not right next door to Buenos Aires.

Bariloche is on a large lake where Argentina and Chile back up on each other. This territory went uncharted for a long time and was only clearly part of Argentina in the late nineteenth century. The early settlers were from Europe, and one good-looking North American cowboy had a very large ranch here. I read about him in a guidebook. Bariloche was very isolated. The nearest town was seventy miles away, and it took two days on horseback to get there.

Once a train reached this mountaintop, Bariloche became a famous ski resort in winter and fishing destination in the summer. Jean-Michel Frank, the famous French decorator, was imported to decorate the giant luxury hotel built here. He came to Buenos Aires regularly before World War II and designed furniture for a company that still manufactures his designs. He fled to Buenos Aires at the time of the war, and then went to New York, where he committed suicide. He was a cousin to Anne Frank of the famous diary. Those were awful times.

The outstanding quality of Bariloche is the light. So clear, so vivid. Each color stands out very sharply. The green of the leaves so very green, the lake so very blue. The sky so clear and crystalline.

We drove up to where the ski resorts thrive. Roads swirl up even higher, and there must be hordes of people here in the wintertime, as the mountainsides are covered with chalets. There is something Swiss about it, true. Unfortunately, there was nothing very "fish" about it.

The fish were absent. Fenil and his brother caught nothing. In my childhood, I often accompanied my grandfather on fishing expeditions, so I am quite used to returning empty-handed except for the fishing pole.

Bariloche is no competition for the Swiss Alps or the Rocky Mountains. The more dramatic skiing may be nearby in Chile. I left Bariloche with many disappointed fishermen still in residence. It does not have the glamour I expected.

What I liked best about Bariloche were the dogs. There are so many of them, largish, black and rust being the principal colors. They're dozing in city streets. Outside of town, every private driveway has a dog sleeping or calmly lying there on guard. Even at night, several are patrolling the city streets, going about their business. Whatever that may be.

They uncannily cross streets and highways, seeming to be able to judge the traffic correctly. They do not appear to be hungry or unkempt. At least not more unkempt than the citizens, who do not seem crazy about shaving, haircuts, general neatness, or cleanliness. But this also has a certain Marie Antoinette air about it, playing at being a simple person. The men are especially unkempt, often with guitar cases. They are almost all certainly of good family and education, exploring the world of the lonely wanderer. They will all be lawyers and bankers later.

Also, everyone young looks very worn. Too many late nights in a boozy town, I guess. Although at night, not many people seem to be about.

Also, there are a great many older people here, in a town where the sidewalks are particularly inhospitable. Lots of holes and steps up and down. Many of the older folks are tourists, I would guess, a bit taken aback at this windy, a little wild, still a frontier kind of town.

The Movie

$\mathbf{P}$hillipe Colmer called me this morning while I was meditating. How old can he be? He was a possibility as a lover for me many years ago. Which never happened. But he has always remained in touch. I remember my friend Babette Bodine saying to me at the time, "What Phillipe doesn't understand is that when you have less to offer, you must do more." I was never quite sure what she meant by "less to offer," if it referred to his financial situation or his personality or his beauty.

Phillipe was supposed to be heterosexual, a young Frenchman who had come to New York to work for a French company, been let go, and then had flung himself upon the flow of opportunities in the city. He was doing fine when I knew him but perhaps expected more attention because he was French. I sensed he needed to be pursued and that was not at all my style. Not then. Not now. At least overtly. He married, and after his divorce I said, "Phillipe, perhaps you should consider a relationship with another man." Standing on that train platform in the morning Connecticut air, he replied, "If it's not going to be you, it's not going to be anyone."

This morning, Phillipe called, which he does irregularly. He had just lost out on a job he had very much hoped to get. How old can he be? He has to be approaching seventy. I told him that these things are meant to be and the more appropriate job would soon be turning up. And reassured him generally as I sat there on the floor on my meditation cushion, a candle flickering in front of my knees.

At the end of our conversation, he said, "Do you remember that night at your apartment when you were massaging my neck?" I didn't, but I said I did. "That was the closest I ever came to changing sides," he said.

"Well, that was meant to be also, Phillipe," I said. I think I wasn't that drawn to him. He was a dark, attractive young man with a lanky French body, but we never kissed. I had no way of knowing if things could be more electric, and they weren't electric enough without the kissing to go any further with our relationship.

I didn't talk to Phillipe about the movie *Broken Sky*, which I had seen for the second time that week. It's called *El Cielo Dividido* in Spanish. It had been directed by Julián Hernández in Mexico. Was it long and tedious, or was it a film that ignored all the Hollywood givens about how to make a movie?

I was bored when I first saw it, and then thought about it a lot the next day. I saw this movie for the first time at the film festival in Montevideo, Uruguay. The gay film festival. It must be the largest international activity in Uruguay. Ten days. Three theaters. Two or three movies a day in each theater. A lot of movies. And a lot of people from Germany, Mexico, the United States. Including me. I appeared in two movies that were in the festival. One is a documentary about my preparation for one of my one-man musicals. It had pretty good attendance, but I had called and invited almost everyone I knew there. Fenil came with me and his little boy. Fenil is not at all abashed about appearing with me at gay events, and his child is too young to have any idea where he is except that there are a lot of people and it's fun and he is the only child in attendance.

Interestingly, when you go to a gay bar in Montevideo, it is generally for both men and women. Both gay men and lesbians are assembled there, which is very unlike the United States. And they all dress very much alike. Boots and jeans and dark, zipper-front jackets. They all have very much the same length hair. And none of them stand out in the world of Montevideo. It is like the 1950s there.

Homosexuality is sort of under the radar. That's the Latin American world. A man isn't gay as long as he doesn't bottom. As long as you don't bend over, or at least people don't know you do, you're fine.

Which is a curious thing about the movie *Broken Sky*. There is a lot of full frontal male nudity and naked sex scenes, but it is not at all pornographic. Not to me, anyway. It's just the way men do it together. And there seems to be a fair amount of the two lovers topping and bottoming and doing the entire repertoire of male sexual activity. One isn't the "girl" and the other the "boy."

When I saw the movie a second time, after ordering it on Netflix, I think I saw what the director was doing. There is no plot, really. It's just boy meets boy, boy rejects boy, boy doesn't get boy back because he has become involved with another guy. It's not a movie that Hollywood could remake with big-name stars because it's just about being in love, not valuing it enough, and then realizing you lost it and it never happens again. It is kind of goosey and romantic and, of course, when your boyfriend rejects you and goes venturing forth, he never wants you back. Someone else is going to glom onto him immediately if he's as good-looking as Fernando Arrojo, who plays the role of Jonas in the movie. The one who says years later, at the end of the movie, "I never loved anyone else but you."

But in its endless drifty and dreamy way, it does capture the feeling of being in love. The two principal actors do make you feel the excitement and uniqueness of being in love. And when the movie is done, you realize how important that is.

Everyone talks about it, but how many have experienced it? And those who have experienced it, how many have forgotten it, undervalued it, or been so involved with themselves they have been unable to care about anyone else?

And so with Fenil and Peter. Where will this go? There is no reason to make a decision between them. Their reasons for needing me are quite different from my reasons for needing them. They need me for the support it gives their physical lives. I need them for the support it gives my emotional life. Each morning when I get up, it is with the realization that I am extraordinarily lucky to be involved with these men on a level beyond fantasy. They really are in my life. I really am in their lives. For someone whose life has essentially been about being in love, this is extremely good fortune.

A Theme of Death

There is a theme of death in my life, beginning with my father's death when I was twelve. Continuing with the loss of my nephew Nicky when I was probably twenty-four. Then Mischa Michelescu . . . the beautiful dark-eyed, dark-curly-haired Mischa Michelescu when I must have been approaching forty. And now that I am between seventy-five and eighty, the deaths begin to cascade.

I think perhaps we die because those relationships, those loves, those dependencies are torn from us until we no longer have enough structure in our bodies and lives to continue. We crumble and fall.

There is something unfair about the deaths of others. There is no escaping from the deaths of others, and yet each is so damaging, so life altering, that even one death can distort your life forever. And each subsequent death twists and tortures our lives into shapes we never planned and never wished to experience. Perhaps those who live to be the oldest are those who have felt the least for others. They have lived untampered with and undistorted by the losses of love.

My father died of shame, really, that he had not been able to take care of his family properly in the Depression. But I don't think he could have taken care of us properly, Depression or no Depression. He was a horsy, handsome man who, even though very much a man's man, lacked confidence and was sunk in personal depression. I remember intensely how his skin smelled. Not sweet, not sour, not sweaty, just his skin. The smell of skin, perhaps presaging the smell of death. When skin rots, and finally, there's nothing to be ashamed of. In the Depression, no matter what happened to you, there was no shame in not surviving. Which he didn't.

What will it be like finally? I think it will be nothing. Just disintegrating into dust and returning to the stars. Like when I was small and sleeping on that "sleeping porch" in Michigan, and the tall trees that lined the streets would be tossing in high winds and I could see the starry sky beyond them and I imagined my bed whirling off into the stars as I fell asleep. Death could be like that. Or it could be like hurrying to meet someone you love. When I was so very much in love with the great love of my life, I was in a taxi hurrying homeward to meet him in the black, wet night of a New York winter, surrounded by the wet metal sides of other cars and taxis, the red and green and white lights of the city streets, the glistening pavement, and filled with the need to be with him. A beautiful moment like that would be suitable for death.

> "I was a nice person once, wasn't I, Eloise?"
>
> J. D. Salinger,
> "Uncle Wiggily in Connecticut"

I was a nice person once, too. I don't think other people can imagine what it means to still be a decent person, if not a nice one, who, at seventy-seven, was never disappointed by life and who hasn't slipped into mind-dulling fantasies about what his life was like. I know no peers. I know no one else like myself except in literature. Thank God for literature.

Everyone seems to be taking a very long time in their dying. It should be briefer, as it is with animals. I so much admire my aunt Katherine, who remained hale until she approached her 101st birthday. Then she sickened and died and was gone in two weeks. The way a pet cat or loved dog might go. She did not eat the heart out of others in her going.

My brother; my ex-lover; my friend Barbara, to whom I felt so close with so little reason to; my friend from opera-dancing days who was never a friend then, but now is because when he calls we live again in the lost 1950s life. All of them seem to be taking a very long time in their dying. Having four people tearing at you with either their need for your concern or your need to be concerned leaves little time or strength for anything else. Yet one must devote a lot of time and strength to other things to keep their drain at arm's length.

In your seventies, there is a tendency to feel like the climber stranded in a hammock on a cliffside in a freezing snowstorm calling his wife in Paris on his cell phone to say good-bye. I, too, feel my chances of emerging alive from the storm of life are nil.

God is being very good and generous to me. It makes me nervous.

As my friend Herb lies dying, I think my life has been pointless but amusing in comparison to others I see. Which are also pointless but not amusing. Even painful. Whose lives do have point? And how many are amusing? Churchill? Columbus? Alexander the Great? From my Zen studies I know that whatever my life is, it is extremely peripheral to what is going on here.

I don't think I have the patience to live another twenty years. People behave so foolishly and against their own best interests, and they cannot behave any other way. They are as programmed as a cage full of monkeys. No wonder Stephen Sondheim called Ethel Merman "The Talking Dog." Indeed.

One morning at seventy-five, I woke up and for the first time was frightened for the future. Not of death but of the real boredom everyone feels on hearing of someone else's death. The resentment families feel when they have to take responsibility for the elderly. Very few people are so charming and interesting that we really want to know them and mourn their passing.

When they had the heat wave in Paris in 2005 and many old people died in their sweltering, airless apartments, they had to get refrigerated trucks to store the bodies, and many people did not return from vacation to claim their relatives until their vacation time ended on the first of September. And many did not come to claim their ancient kin at all.

The man I once loved more than I have ever loved anyone else is dying in Philadelphia. Yet he calls and wants me to buy him a car to replace the old one he has been driving for twenty years. I want to say, "Wait a minute. I thought you were dying." But I don't.

I have sent him quite a lot of money for medicines and bills and now wonder if he is really dying. Or is this a hoax to conjure money from me? He is Italian. Anything is possible. One must maintain an open mind so as not to think badly of oneself later. Perhaps he is going or has gone mad with the imminence of his death. He has seen life as something to be used, as a spoiled, handsome child does. Now it is using him. When we were in the thick of our relationship, he would say, "You're the only one I kiss."

Panama

It was pissing down rain in Panama City. Rainy season. Who knew? No one ever goes to Panama from Miami. All you know about it is that middle-class Americans from the Midwest go there to retire in gated communities as much like Illinois as possible. Middle, middle, middle.

But Fenil wanted to meet there. Direct flights flew to Panama from where he was and from where I was. And it was cold where he was and hot where I was.

I had to fit it into a tight schedule, as I was going to go to Europe to spend time with Peter. That had been booked for a long time, and there was no changing it. But I had been missing Fenil a lot. Strange. Someone becomes the person in your life whether you have decided upon it or not. And there you are.

We met in a seventy-story hotel in Panama. When I arrived in the room, there was a scrawled note on my bed. "I am at the pool." Fenil loves these kinds of places. The pools, the gyms, the little restaurants, the room service.

Fenil is ahead of his years. He is only twenty-six but has lived much more than twenty-six years. He is always taken to be older than he is. Partly because of the way he carries his body: very self-assured. Partly because of his voice: low and manly. Usually men don't realize that life isn't the same year repeating itself until they reach the age of twenty-eight. They then realize that they are aging and steps must be taken that life doesn't pass unheeded. Fenil is already there and recently has become more involved in keeping his body fit. At hotels and beaches he swims a lot and is in the gym every day. He is an early riser, which I am not, but I accompany him to the gym frequently if it isn't too early.

I went to join him at the pool, which was a vertiginous cliff's-edge body of water on the thirteenth floor of the hotel. All the time I was in Panama City I felt like a bird in flight paused on quivering branches high in the air. Our room was on the seventeenth floor with a balcony hanging high. I cannot imagine relaxing or sunbathing so far up in the air without a hint of dizzying vertigo hovering about me. And yet stories and stories reached above me, with people evidently quite at ease on their balconies, at the height where small planes go.

This is the twenty-first century. What everyone assumes is all right to do is what everyone does without question. Why would they put balconies on the seventieth floor if it wasn't all right? And to be fair, you never hear of anyone tumbling from a high hotel balcony. Or rarely.

Fenil was lying beside the pool and immediately got up. "I knew you must be somewhere around. I was starting to get a hard-on," he said. He often made these provocative remarks. I cannot say that I disliked them.

"Would you rather go to the room or have lunch?" I said. There was a very open-air restaurant between the two pools on this high bird perch.

"I think I'd rather eat at the moment," he said. He had flown overnight. I had called the hotel and asked that he be allowed to go to the room even though he was to arrive early in the morning. They had been very hospitable, he said. Some hotels hadn't been so accommodating to this handsome young man in other cities, and he hadn't liked it.

Eating lunch, we looked out over the skyscraper-jammed horizon of Panama City. Something is going on in Panama, I'm not quite sure what, but there is a lot of money there. The hotel was tightly locked in on both sides by sister skyscrapers going up, both in midconstruction. Workmen were scampering over both of them, munching sandwiches on railless balconies high above us. Leaning out of windows perilously to screw in this or adjust that. You had to have no sense of where you are to do what they were doing. One man was standing on a folding ladder doing something to a balcony ceiling light. If the ladder had tipped, he would have fallen some twenty stories. He was oblivious to this. It made it hard for me to eat lunch.

Panama City is a place with little past. It was just a squalor-laden little dump in the times when the Panama Canal was owned by the United States. Once turned over to the Panamanian government, the canal's earnings of some four million dollars a day made a lot of difference. Thirty to forty ships a day go through the canal: Pacific to Atlantic in the morning, Atlantic to Pacific in the afternoon. Ships pay up to $450,000 for their passage, according to their size and cargo. But that can't account for the *frenesi* of building here. The city compares favorably to Miami in visual impact. What are all these buildings for? Are there a lot of banks here? Drug money is what immediately comes to mind, my being from Miami.

In retrospect, now that the Panama adventure is over, spending this time with Fenil in some ways reprised my former lovers. There were three, and each of them was brought very much to mind as I spent this time with Fenil.

I always thought I would have four major romances in my life. Four, fourteen, and forty-four are numbers that repeatedly surface for me. And this period in my life seems to be concerning itself with the question, who is to be number four? Will there be a number four? Am I just theatricalizing my private life into this foursome concept? Perhaps to reassure myself that that there will be a fourth lover this late in my life?

It is very strange, but as I get older, I feel more and more that I am on an earth that is a revolving, self-sustaining spaceship—going where? And for what purpose? I know the answers people give themselves are only for self-assurance, and we can never know the answer. No more than I can explain to my cat that the world is round can I comprehend what I am doing here. But I do feel we all have destinies. I am convinced that we must somehow give ourselves over to these destinies and not fight them. Out of fear, many people get off the train of life at the wrong station: the wrong marriage, the wrong career, the wrong town. Courage is what carries us forward. And these men have been my destiny, and I have had the courage to involve myself with them and also the courage to leave them.

Fenil triggers thoughts of Clyde, my first real lover. Clyde wasn't really homosexual. Well, perhaps there was part of him that was. More, I think he was capable of falling in love with someone and not being that concerned about their plumbing. Fenil is like that. He said to me, "I'm not usually interested in other men, but you're for me."

Clyde and I met in the navy. I was an officer. He was an enlisted man. A big, blond, brawny but soft-bodied guy. Our ship had come into Honolulu. We had vaguely mentioned meeting ashore. He was one of the men who worked with me in the radio shack aboard the ship where I was the communications officer. When I returned to the ship later that day and went to the radio shack he was there. He turned and, looking at me intensely, said, "I looked everywhere for you, but I couldn't find you." We went out on the little exterior deck beside the shack and held hands. He was crying. I started to cry, too.

The sun was setting as we steamed out past Diamond Head promontory. It was pretty intense. When we arrived in San Francisco, I was reassigned to an admiral's staff in San Diego; he went to another ship. We met in various West Coast ports and our romance became increasingly sexual. We were both discharged about a year later, only one month apart, our terms of duty having been completed.

Clyde was always distressed about his relationship with me yet often instigated sexual contact. He would have sex with me, and then cry for his mother. And then be riding in the back of someone's car with me and take my hand and put it on his crotch. He wanted it, and he didn't want it.

We went to New York together and spent a summer there before he started college and I pursued a career in advertising. Clyde was only two years younger than I was but had never gone to college. I encouraged him, and he enrolled in a school back home in his midwestern state.

After our three months in New York, living in a tiny, ancient house in Greenwich Village, I felt I could let him go. Although earlier in our relationship I would cling to him and say, "Don't go away. Don't leave me. Not yet. Not yet." I think the loss of my father when I was young, two older brothers who were very unconcerned about me, and a loving grandfather who was nevertheless not very present left me feeling the need of male support. And Clyde certainly was that for me. He was very manly, very easily affectionate, liked being with me (we rarely argued), and perhaps I energized him.

But Clyde's feelings for me were on two levels. First, there was his simply dismissing our sexual similarities and loving me for who I was. What a huge experience for a gay man.

But there was also another layer of sexual interest. He actually wanted male sexual experimentation. He liked what we two did together, and I think that allure frightened him.

And yet my absence of emotional hysteria at his leaving disappointed him. He said, "You don't seem very sorry to see me go." I protested, but I wasn't. I wanted more experientially and romantically than Clyde was bringing to the table. And yet. And yet.

Clyde left on Friday, and I went to Fire Island for the weekend. When I returned to our apartment alone on a Sunday evening I realized he was gone. I was alone. And the full sense of his absence struck me. I felt it.

We spoke frequently on the phone and were assuming he would return to New York the next summer. And then one autumn evening he called to tell me he had fallen in love with his French teacher and was planning to marry her. I put down the phone, and it was as though I had been crossing a long, sunny plain reaching out ahead of me and had suddenly looked down to find I was on the edge of a huge dark canyon I had not seen or expected. There was no way to the other side. That future was no longer available to me.

Clyde and I have remained in touch somewhat through the years. He finished college, then law school, and assumed a position in the legal administration in his state. In his earlier married years we were friendlier. Now he seems distant and embarrassed, and I feel I am only a distant memory. One he regrets. His interest in other men was certainly quashed, although he said to me, "My having known you will help me understand other people in the future." He was a smart man and a good man and fulfilled himself in his own eyes, I am sure. In mine, not completely. But could he have? The one thing he said early in our relationship that I have always carried with me is "If there's no solution, it isn't a problem. It's just a situation." How could he have known that so young?

And so with Fenil, I feel that our relationship is symptomatic of his having emotions, sexual alerts, feelings toward men that can only alarm him. In the Latin American world, a man is not homosexual as long as he is the aggressive partner. But perhaps he has submissive feelings. Perhaps he has interests in penises other than his own. That would disturb Fenil quite a lot. And there I find that deep-seated similarity to Clyde. And what does this similarity have to do with me? Other than my recognizing it?

How much of our relationship with lovers has to do with them and how much has it to do with us? Are there elements in love that are there only to recapitulate themes in our lives?

My rhythm with Fenil was to spend the day with him, and then after dinner, I would go to bed and he would go to the hotel bar if he were somewhere quite unknown like Panama, or out barhopping if we were somewhere better known to him like Buenos Aires.

In Panama, I began to feel he was looking forward to his night freedom more each day, so one evening I said to him, "Come on, I'll go to the bar with you." When the bartender asked what I was drinking I said, "I'll have an Old-Fashioned." This was a drink we often had those many years ago when I was in the navy and during my early time in New York with Clyde. And I probably hadn't had a cocktail since then. I was being funny, but the bartender, a middle-aged black man, didn't bat an eye. He wrote it on his pad. Fenil ordered the same thing. When the drink came, it was about twice the size of the drink we had back in the mid-twentieth century, but otherwise identical. Did anyone still drink Old-Fashioneds back in the United States or were there still traveling businessmen drifting through the hotel, continuing to drink their long-accustomed Old-Fashioneds?

Fenil said after the first one, "You're just coming to the bar to keep me from being here by myself, aren't you?"

"Of course," I said. "Should we have another one?" We did, and I felt very little from it although I drink nothing but wine, and that only with meals. Not because I have ever had a drinking problem. I am not at all addictive. But I don't want to ruin my looks, which smoking and drinking do faster than anything else. And it really isn't vanity but more not wanting to be left out by life.

Anyway, I went to bed. Fenil accompanied me, kissed me good night, and went his way. When he returned he was always exceptionally quiet, but I would wake up and notice by the bedside clock that it would be 1:30 or 2:00 in the morning. His late arrivals actually worked for us, as I sleep a lot, Fenil doesn't, and in this way, we get up about the same time: around 9:00.

The next morning I had agreed to meet him at the pool after his gym workout. There were two pools high in the hotel, and I went to the one reserved for hotel guests. Fenil didn't show up after a long wait. I went down to the gym. He was long gone, they said. I went back up to the pool reserved for the residents of the apartments higher up in the hotel building. He was in the pool chatting up a blonde woman as they both hugged the edge of the pool.

"Oh, there you are," I said sociably. "I was waiting for you at the other pool. I'll see you back at the room." When he returned he said the blonde woman was in Panama selling hospital equipment and was there with her boyfriend. I asked myself, did I care and why did I care?

That night I woke intermittently to find Fenil hadn't returned at 2:00 or at 4:00. He finally came even more stealthily than usual at 5:30. I said nothing about it, lying in bed and reading until he woke up sometime after 10:00.

Some actions change a relationship permanently. Fenil was certainly not at the bar until five o'clock in the morning. It was a kind of failure to me that affected deeply how I felt about him. And I thought of how my lover Frederick, my second great romance, had failed me in the same way.

This was in that unlikely part of my life when I was dancing at the opera in New York. I lied about my age, pretending I was a good bit younger than I was. My looks let me get away with it. And I had great legs. Have. The other boys in the dressing room used to say, "They shouldn't try to make you dance. They should let you just go out and walk around."

Frederick was tall, handsome, and also had great legs. There was a time when he was said to be the handsomest man in New York. Like me, he was an apprentice dancer with the ballet company. I think we became lovers because he had nowhere to live and moved in with me in my cold-water flat in Chelsea.

Those were almost unbelievable days compared to the New York of today. Four rooms, no heat but water and a gas-fueled kitchen stove that, if you left the oven door open, could very adequately heat three of the four rooms in cold weather. There was a big front room, and I just closed the door to it when the temperature dropped. A bathtub stood in the kitchen with an enamel cover: up when you bathed, down when you were preparing meals. The toilet was in the hall. What's the definition of a bachelor? Someone who pees in the sink. And there was a sink in the corner of the kitchen. The rent was twenty-five dollars a month. I had a friend who paid nine dollars for two rooms on the Lower East Side.

Frederick and I had become friendly in a kind of a trio with another dancer, Florian. We hung out together until I shepherded Frederick aside as my own property.

At some point, in a moment of friendly feeling, I had told Florian I was actually twenty-six, not twenty-two. Once I had Frederick in my bed, Florian went to the director of the opera ballet and told him. Suddenly there was less promise there than met the eye, and I was called in and dismissed. From the company, from the school, from the opera. I was knocked for a loop. Shattered. My whole life was going to the opera at ten each morning, rehearsing until four in the afternoon, going to ballet class until seven (two classes if possible), when I reported to the dressing rooms to prepare for that evening's production. Six days a week. We did matinees on Saturday, too. On Sunday, I was usually rehearsing with some modern dance group for a concert. It was a full life, and I loved it. Suddenly . . . *Bam!* . . . It was gone. It was another one of those crossings of the desert to suddenly find a great engulfing canyon at my feet.

I rushed back to the cold-water flat to tell Frederick. He wasn't there. He never appeared that afternoon or that evening or all night long. I suffered a lot. Really. My life had fallen completely apart, and the man I loved wasn't there. By morning, I had become calmer. And a kind of insurmountable wall had built up between Frederick and me. We were together pretty much for another thirty years, but that wall never came down, and I never climbed over it. He had failed me.

When he came in shortly after dawn, he explained he had spent the night with a Japanese friend whom he had met at a swimming pool in Greenwich Village a year or so before. He said, "If you think I am big, you should see Yamamoto. [Or Hidiyoki or whoever it was.] He's twice as big as I am." And for Frederick, that would always be a very good reason for being out of touch and failing to appear.

And so it was with Fenil. When I suggested several days later that he had spent the night with the blonde woman from the pool, he said, "Oh, don't be childish." For Fenil, having sex with a woman is a perfectly reasonable thing to do that had absolutely nothing to do with me. And why I would think it did escaped him completely.

Often if I made a comment that didn't please him he would say, "You're just saying that because you're jealous." My jealousy seemed to him out of line and silly and ridiculous. Actually, I think he's right, but the wall went up that night. The wall of feeling that I could not count on him. I had come to feel resolutely that he was the only person with whom I did not feel alone. I have friends, and I enjoy their company, but within me there is always a distance from them. Only with Fenil did I not feel that way. But now, the wall had gone up.

A day or so after Fenil spent the night out, we were having breakfast at the hotel and the blonde woman was at a nearby table, looking intently at her computer. Fenil took no notice of her or she of him. Their failure to greet one another said more to me than if they had spoken.

And so it is with Fenil. There are parts of his life that are none of my business. He does not lie about them. He may gloss over them or give me a bit of information so I can forget about it. But there is certainly much going on. And so, perhaps this allocating part of his life to me is how he is linked to Mark, my third lover, and until now, the great love of my life.

People ask me if Mark was my lover before or after Frederick, and I say, "During." It was true. For ten years, Mark and I had the romance that fulfilled me and allows me to feel that I have experienced what I wished to in my life. But I was involved with Frederick at the same time. You tell me.

I never wanted a domestic relationship. I didn't want my feelings for someone stretched and trodden upon and distorted through endless repetition and regimes of meals and laundry and bedmaking. That I take care of myself. When I am with the person I love I do not want to discuss who left wet bath towels on the bathroom floor. And so it was with Mark. A talented actor, dancer, singer whom I met when I was managing a ballet school for an important ballet company. Yes, that's another career of mine. Does that make six or seven?

Mark was ten years younger than I was. It was our sexual interfacing that left me wanting nothing more.

I think our bodies and our minds have two completely different agendas. I think we can stumble upon someone of great compatibility, similar interests, and similar sleep patterns. So important if you are going to live with someone if they leap out of bed at five in the morning and you stumble out at ten. But this is only to say, for me, compatibility is like roommates with a little sex thrown in. And, of course, with heterosexual couples in a marriage or a long-term relationship, it is just about getting along and not being lonely. Not about the conflagration when two bodies have something to say to one another.

And when those bodies collide, it has so much more meaning than the long years of amiability. When bodies collide, the minds within can accept that the other mind within may have little companionship to offer. Your intellects, your backgrounds, your educations may have little meaning for each other and you may be so different that it eventually destroys the meaning of the bodily collision. But the bodily collisions are essential or you feel that you never loved. Never lived.

Is that all there is? The singer Peggy Lee's lament is, I think, the song of someone whose body hasn't met the right body. Which is all to explain Mark.

As I always said, "When he fucked you, you stayed fucked for a while." He needed you, he wanted you, he gave everything over to you.

For many men, intercourse is just a small step above masturbation. Sometimes not even that. Because the other person is just the equivalent of some kind of blow-up sex toy. Mark wasn't like that. It was definitely you.

And as I have frequently said, "Crazy people can be great in bed." Which was true of Mark, who made great advances in his theater career in his twenties. Then he got in his own way so much in his thirties that he destroyed what he had achieved. The arguments with directors, refusing roles, alienating management. I felt this "stepping in your own knickers" kind of behavior was an expression of fear. The fear of not being able to handle true stardom. Am I good enough? Do I deserve it? These kinds of questions, I think, often destroy careers more than lack of opportunity.

When I was forty and Mark was thirty, I realized I would have to go crazy with him, see the world in the same distorted way he did, or leave. And I left.

But while we were in our bodily relating ten years together, I knew little of many areas of Mark's life. "You are the only one I kiss," he would say. He loved the attention he often got from celebrities, and I am sure he felt he owed it to himself as well as them to come as close as he could get to them. And this is something you have to accept. In no way could I have ever wanted or expected any kind of domestic life with Mark.

He died not long ago, spending most of his later life as a waiter, and then being an invalid with a bad back (he claimed). If I would have stayed with him, I would have been dead many years ago, which is in no way to denigrate what he gave to my life. I felt a completion and nothing greater to experience through being with him. I think this is something that gay men frequently miss out on. Life shortchanges them into brief, meaningless encounters that are akin to shopping in a meat market. It leaves them sour and dissatisfied. Perhaps completion is a matter of luck or being sensitive to your destiny. I do not know.

I do know that this is the link to Fenil. I think the body collision is there. The lives our minds lead are essentially very different.

And when you review the men you have loved, you have to wonder to what degree your life dictated those choices. How much of it is seeking the love your family didn't give you? For gay men, it's the father who was absent emotionally and whose love was just as important as the love of your mother.

When I was dancing, I remember getting aboard the Seventh Avenue subway in New York, which delivered me directly to the opera's stage door. As I sat down and the train pulled away, I realized that I had loved my father very much. The realization was like some gigantic bank vault door slamming shut. *Wham!*

My poor father, whom I was always ignored by or in conflict with. My brothers, and particularly my sister, were much more comfortable with him. He was one to quickly reach out and strike his children. I was the only one to fight back.

So was it this unfinished love I was seeking to fulfill with my loves? And how is it after all these years that I am still here, undefeated, full of emotion and enthusiasm, waiting for Fenil?

Or is it something even bigger? Something essential to life that we want to be one with another living being? The urge behind breeding, or is it actually an urge not to be left alone out here in the stars?

They Let Me
Cry Myself to Sleep

I was in ballet class last night, and we were stretching on the floor as the class began. I was lying down pulling my straightened leg up toward my chest. I was holding my calf pulling it down and suddenly was very aware that it was warm and smooth and strong. My legs have always been one of my best features. Or is that two? (When I was playing the role of a drag queen serial killer I wore a denim miniskirt. On opening night I passed the box office guy on my way into the theater, and he yelled out, "You got a great pair of stems.")

So back to ballet class . . . I realized that before too much longer this flesh of mine will be decaying underground. Or will be consumed by fire, and then will sit around as ashes in a vase somewhere. And as I pulled, I thought of Fenil's warm, strong body in my arms and that it is gone forever also and I wanted to cry. I haven't yet. But there on the floor of that big, empty, mirrored room, surrounded by other dancers, I wanted to cry and cry and cry.

Many years ago, my mother told me that when I was a baby they were having dinner downstairs and heard me crying in my room. I cried without ceasing, and they decided to just let me cry myself out. Which I finally did. After dinner, they went upstairs to check on me and found that my baby legs had become entangled in my blanket and I couldn't lower them to the bed. And they felt terribly guilty.

I was the third child. They were in the suddenly terrifying depths of the big Depression of the 1930s. Another child was probably not wanted, and they had had a surfeit of children crying upstairs, I am sure, with my two older brothers, who were not much older. Even so.

This deeply embedded and never-ending need that I have for someone like Fenil must, in part, stem from being homosexual and also in part from being a small child in a family where they could just leave you to cry yourself to sleep. I needed warmth and reassurance and affection and certainly I did receive it. But not enough. Not enough. And now with Fenil disappearing from my life, that same need reappears. And I am left to cry myself to sleep.

Driving through the Stars

The poet John Wieners wrote, "The beauty of men never dies. It drives a blue car through the stars."

If I thought dying was like rushing to meet a handsome lover, a lover who truly loves you as you do him, who will hold you in his arms and bring you to orgasm in the most thrilling manner, I'd be willing to die without a qualm. I think I will start thinking of death in that way. Start thinking of God as the handsome lover waiting for me out there in the stars.

I think homosexuals love in a way women can but often don't. We perhaps respond sexually to other men, and only sexually, when we are younger. But if you are at all enterprising and have any kind of sense, by the time you're in your early twenties you've done that enough.

And nature, in its clumsy way, swings someone into view who is really no handsomer or more special than many others, but you find a little bell rings. And if you're lucky, the bell rings for both of you.

And if it doesn't ring for him, it does one day because you love him.

Which brings us to domesticity. The idea that the domestic life of Mom, Dad, and the kids spells happiness is very recent historically. It wasn't until Queen Victoria's time that this was considered a desirable goal. Before her time, happiness was probably spelled out as fame, power, riches, sex with beautiful people. Happiness at home never came up.

Then Victoria wed and bred and set a royal example of domestic bliss for everyone to follow, which now even homosexual men and women wish to copy. I recently saw daguerreotypes of some of Victoria's

126

children. They were all gussied up, standing in what looked like the gardens of Windsor Castle on an overcast day. What days aren't overcast in England? Only the ones when it's raining.

The royal little girls were decorated with plumes, tight gloves, stiff-hooped and ruffled skirts, albeit only down to their knees. Their brother was in kilts and an awkward Scottish hat that I'm sure he hated wearing. He would not look at the camera and seemed quite downcast. Their looks certainly didn't suggest that home life with Vicky and Al was much of a ball. But somehow, the idea has permeated all of Western society to the point that any deviation from it is looked upon as unfortunate or sinful. How is it that the bourgeois can only conceive of "boring" as a legitimate goal?

Which is only to say that perhaps as you lie under someone's loving body and you fall, fall, fall through your orgasm and call out to him/her, "Hold me, hold me very tight," you are getting your glimpse of heaven. And that is what it will be like when the end comes: falling, falling, falling through the stars into the arms of the one you loved most of all in your whole life in the entire world in the entire universe. And perhaps for some it will be for the first time. How wonderful. It's an idea worth considering.

The Fall of Phaeton

I have a bronze statue by Donald De Lue of the fall of Phaeton, who drove his sky-borne chariot too near the sun. Is that correct? I confuse this myth with the fall of Icarus, whose wings collapsed when the wax that held the feathers in place melted from the sun as he flew higher and higher.

At first I thought my statue was Icarus, and then remembered no horse accompanied him into the air. No, it is Phaeton, who is almost obscured by his plunging horse in my statue. The horse's great rounded buttocks and hindquarters are uppermost; Phaeton, head down, is falling at the horse's side.

I also have a terracotta plaque of the horse and Phaeton falling that is allegedly a sample or maquette for a large-scale wall decoration on the ill-fated *Normandie*, the French liner that finally burned and sank at its pier in New York during World War II. It probably isn't. If all the attributed designs and drawings, examples and samples claimed to have been done for the *Normandie* were, in fact, done for that ship, it would have been ten times bigger than it was.

My terracotta plaque, too, has a dominating, tumbling horse upside down with Phaeton falling beside it. Only very recently did I notice that Phaeton's profile projects below the lower edge of the plaque, almost a jagged triangle jutting down.

Why do I find these falling horses and men so compelling? Perhaps that huge falling expresses the feeling of orgasm. I just read today that the orgasmic seizure of pleasure is the result of dopamine being released into the brain. Yes, my darling, that dark feeling that you are falling out into the stars, falling, falling, falling, calling out to your partner, "Hold me, hold me tight," for fear you'll never stop falling, is just the result of some chemicals suddenly flooding into your little baby head. Disappointing, isn't it? And all the time you thought it was God contacting you. One begins to understand drug addicts, who are forever flooding their systems with chemicals in the hope of capturing something like that feeling.

The article that I read said that some people have low levels of dopamine and have to bungee jump off high bridges or climb skyscrapers with their bare hands just to experience the thrill. So maybe those people who are after sex, sex, sex all the time are the ones who don't have the great orgasms. People like myself, who don't have a lot of sex, sex, sex anymore, would like to think that anyway.

So there you have it. The orgasm. Falling through space and time, not far from the great curving butt of a horse, not unlike the great, curving butts so admired by men who love men.

Last Notes on
the Theme of Death

Suddenly death seems omnipresent. It began with a friend of Peter's coming to Montevideo to buy a house. He did so. Then installed himself in it and lay in bed drinking vodka until his family had to put him in a hospital, from which he walked out early one morning and threw himself in the river.

Then Mark died after lots of different illnesses. Ten years younger than I am. I had to go and empty the house I had bought him and put it up for sale. He had kept every postcard I had ever sent him. His mother's purse stood on the coffee table, although she had died ten years earlier. It was awful.

Then my big dog Bibi died. She was aged and had cancer and died in my arms when the vet euthanized her, but that was awful, too. Her constant barking at the slightest passerby and scrambling about like an ungainly card table had filled the house with much more life than I realized.

And then upon my return from Europe, I had a letter telling me my longtime school friend Sally was gone. She had slipped into forgetfulness but was apparently healthy when we last spoke on the phone. She kept saying, "You sound so familiar," and I would reply, "Jesus Christ, Sally, we've known each other for more than half a century. Go to the mantel and look at the pictures. See the man in white? That's me!" And she would do so, carrying her mobile phone, and say, "You look so familiar," and then we would laugh. Like two strangers who liked each other.

All this death. It makes you think. It makes you think.

My Cat and the Abbott

My cat crawled upon my chest this morning as I was awakening. He is very old. Fifteen going on sixteen. He is from France. His name is Harry.

Harry is a thin tiger cat whose eyes are somewhat sunken. As he purred and peered into my face, I thought, *Harry is so old that he likes to lie upon my body and feel the fact that he is in contact with another living body. In that way, he knows that he is alive himself.*

Looking into his eyes, I noticed they seemed black and empty. Like holes. And I remembered facing the Abbott during a long meditation session in New York when I was very involved with my Zen studies. It was perhaps at night during a tiring weekend. Looking at the Abbott's Asian face in the darkened room, it was as though I were looking through his eyes into the night sky. And if I were to come close and peer through that masklike face, I would see all the stars and constellations strewn across the midnight blue sky. It suddenly seemed very big in that little room.

I am very glad to have had that experience. I would not like to do it as a regular thing. Once in an individual conference with the Abbott, discussing why one meditated, I said, "I'm not sure I want to be one with the universe."

He replied, "You don't have a thing to worry about."

Just Shut Up

Sometimes I just want to tell myself, "Why don't you just shut up?" I'll hear myself at dinner or lunch or at a party dealing out all my ideas about how people waste their lives and pursue the wrong goals and what they should really be doing and how they should really be living, and I'm witty and it all sounds so new and fresh and startling to the people I'm talking to, and they say things like, "Do other people think the way you do?" And I sound like some sort of mechanical doll. I've heard myself say these things so many times.

And I suddenly flashed on a symbolic scene. It is in the countryside, and over a slow rise come a cavalcade of cars, all on the detour of life. And there I am on the corner. They can go straight ahead, or they can take the turn that I am standing there indicating. And I suddenly drop my arm and let them proceed.

And I think, *Go ahead. Go straight ahead to fat legs and bald spots. To arguing with children who don't like you, and, truth be told, you don't like them very much. What's to like?*

Just go straight ahead to paltry decor in the suburbs or jammed into high rises. Go straight ahead to bad art, bad fashion, bad bodies. Darlings, be my guests. Step into the trap, believe all the hooey, because finally, you're not smart enough or brave enough to ever find out who you are, and then put a life together that will ever let you feel fulfilled.

Yesterday, I got up to go to the bathroom just as the sun was rising, and I thought of the routine of the sun forever coming up, the world eternally turning, the boring inevitability of it all. Why don't other people get bored with it? What's so bad about dying? Imagine the horror of listening to Mozart forever.

I Really Loved It

On the night flight back from Montevideo, I looked out the window. The plane's wing made a wide silvery sweep into the night. Above, there was a great white moon and the air was navy blue. Down below, the clouds of the Amazon jungle were like small whipped-cream mountaintops. I thought, *If I were to fall out of the plane right this moment, down, down through the dark blue air in the moonlight, I wouldn't be afraid. I would only think I had a great time while I was here. I really loved it. I really loved it. I really loved it.* Splat.

My Nude

I was photographed nude by Dimitris Yeros to illustrate a Cavafy poem for his new book. He posed me in an armchair in my living room. Behind me and around me perched three much younger men in the nude, each very handsome. My dancer's feet extended into the foreground in their knobbiness. Otherwise, I looked pretty good. I tucked my private parts away. This is the poem:

> It is the joy and consolation of my life
> To remember the caresses, the kisses of those loves
> That were my fulfillment.
> It is the joy and consolation of my life,
> I, who never wanted the boring little loves
> The rest of you have.

As I write this, I wonder if Dimitris chose this poem particularly for me. I hadn't thought of it before, but it expresses much of what I feel—*except it isn't quite time to look back yet.*